EVEN
IN
Death

A Short Story Collection

By Kristy Feltenberger Gillespie
2014

KEEP CALM PUBLISHING

Keep Calm Publishing
P.O. Box 3477
Warrenton, VA 20188

www.kristyfgillespie.com

Acknowledgments

Patrick, for always encouraging me to write "my stories."

My mom, dad, brother, Grandma and Pa Feltenberger, and Grandma and Pap Petrunak for being my support system.

My friends, especially The Sarcastic Broads Club, members of Write By the Rails, Gary, Claudia, Terry, Tammy, Sharon, Carrie, Kelly, Peg, Karen, Danielle, and Megan.

"A Flower Story" is dedicated to John, my co-worker and friend. Thanks for planting that seed in my head.

"What's Really There" is dedicated to my parents who reside with ghosts.

Editor Katherine Mercurio Gotthardt

Illustrator Karri Klawiter

Model Stock Photographer Rebecca Röske

Feather Stock Photographer Maple Rose

TABLE OF CONTENTS

A FINE WINTER DAY   1

A FLOWER STORY   13

LOOSE ENDS   19

SCRAMBLED EGG   39

THE COLLECTOR   49

WHAT'S REALLY THERE   59

KAYANNA PEPPER   75

EVEN IN DEATH   87

MOTIVATOR   99

WHAT CAUGHT MY SENSES   111

NOTES   133

ABOUT KRISTY FELTENBERGER GILLESPIE   134

A Fine Winter Day

My twin sister Corinne enters our bedroom clutching five gift boxes overflowing with khaki pants and bulky sweaters. She drops them on our coffee stained carpet before adding her red leather jacket, matching gloves, and purple Doc Marten boots to the heap. I fling the pens and torn notebook papers that were scattered across my unmade bed as a gesture for her to sit down.

Corinne embraces the stuffed reindeer which is a gift from our uncle. Uncle Ted is a hoarder and auction addict; therefore all twenty-eight family members receive an identical Christmas and birthday gift from him each year. Two days prior we celebrated Christmas at Grandma and Pap's. Corinne spent most of the day huddled in Pap's recliner, clutching that reindeer. Our relatives assumed she was suffering from monthly cramps or a nasty stomach bug. It helps that one doesn't have to try too hard to disappear in a large family.

Before I have a chance to ask how she is, she snaps, "Chloe, I'm fine."

I nod and toy with the gaudy ring on my left pointer finger. "Can I make you a cup of tea? It always makes me feel better." Crap, what an incredibly stupid thing to say. She doesn't have a sore throat for crying out loud.

"No, what I need is a cigarette." She riffles through her purse which reeks of smoke and cheap perfume. With shaking fingers she lights a Marlboro Light.

I almost comment on how pissed our mother and stepfather will be if they smell smoke, but I light a peach scented incense stick instead.

"Are those gifts from Jack?" I ask.

Corinne glares at me.

"I'm sorry, that was another stupid thing to say."

"Yes, they're from Jack. Evidently Jack assumed that clothes from J.C. Penney would cheer me up. What am I, seventy and spending the holiday in Aspen? The only thing that's cheering me up is this cigarette. He doesn't allow anyone to smoke in his precious truck."

"Corinne, I'm so sorry." I reach out to stroke her long, tangled hair but she swats my hand away.

"What have you done all day?" She brushes a tear from her eye and slowly exhales smoke.

"I remained in our room writing crappy poetry and sleeping. It was boring."

"It sure beats my day."

"What was it like?"

"I really don't want to talk about it." She drops the cigarette butt into a cold cup of coffee.

There is a rap on our bedroom door. I spray CK One perfume to mask the lingering smoke.

"I really don't want to speak to her either," Corinne mutters.

I open the door a crack.

"Chloe, how are you feeling?" My mother's arms are folded tightly and the muscles in her jaw twitch.

"I'm fine."

"Would you like some tea?"

I shake my head. Why was she asking me if I needed tea? I was fine.

"Make sure you rest." She opens her mouth as if to say more but turns away instead.

I ease the door closed and glance at the clock which reads 7:00 pm.

Mother Love Bone blares from the speakers and Corinne sings along. "Chloe don't know better. Chloe's just like me, only beautiful."

In turn, I start to cry, and Corrine comforts me. "I'm fine but I'll tell you everything if it will make you feel better," she says. She hands me a fistful of clean tissues and rubs my back in rhythmic circles.

"I would have gone with you." I sniff.

"I know, but I didn't want both of us to suffer with Jack for six hours in a confined space." She laughs bitterly. "I hope to never see him again."

"Was he an ass?"

"He is an ass. In fact, he asked if I wanted to go to a basketball game tonight, unbelievable." She rolls her eyes while more tears form. "And after the procedure we stopped at a diner because the ass was hungry and fast food wasn't up to par. It was cold in the truck, so I sat across from him in the tattered booth, cramping and bleeding. While he dipped nugget after nugget in honey mustard sauce; I imagined plucking the steak knife from the man adjacent from us and stabbing Jack through his shriveled heart. I suppose it's mainly my fault because I should have realized from the get go what a spoiled little boy he is."

"He seemed charming, at least in the beginning. However, as time went on, I didn't like how cocky he was; as if going to school to be a physician's assistant is right up there with brain surgery. And I didn't like how he teased us for majoring in psychology. And the fact he gave you morning after pills a week later. What an idiot," I say.

She laughs. "I'm returning the gifts I bought him from American Eagle. The procedure was four hundred dollars and he didn't offer a dime." She bites her lip and shakes her head slowly.

"Bastard." I light two cigarettes.

"Well, it's over."

"Did it hurt? Are you in pain?" I ask.

"I wish I was in pain for doing such a horrible, selfish, evil thing. But it only feels like a heavy period."

"Thank God you're ok. I kept glancing at the clock all day. Where did you have to go that it took so long?"

"We drove to Maryland because that was the closest place. I wanted the day to be frigid and gray but it was clear and crisp and beautiful, at least on the trip there." Corinne sighs.

The only part of winter we like is the brief exhilaration of wind whipping through our skin, muscle, and bone like shards of ice ricocheting off of withered tree branches. We think of spring as a bipolar season, summer as manic, fall as anxious and winter as melancholy.

"Were there any protesters?" I ask.

"No, and the building was nondescript like a post office. However, we had to be buzzed in and there was a plastic partition at the receptionist's desk and it was smudged with fingerprints. She made me pay even before I finished filling out the paperwork. And then we sat in the grungy waiting room."

"Were there a lot of couples there?"

"No, most of the women were alone. I expected to see a lot of young girls but there were older women there, too."

"Wow, that surprises me."

"After an eternity sitting next to the ass, who kept making snide remarks about the various cautionary signs concerning STDs; I was summoned one step closer on my quest to see the wizard.

I peed in a plastic container and held it up to the light. I noticed how gold and cloudy it was. I really need to drink more water. Regardless, a few minutes later a stocky woman in scrubs whose name tag read 'Bonnie B.' announced I was pregnant. Duh. Then I was forced to speak to Counselor Brandy who looked like she was twelve. Her office was so small our knees nearly touched. She asked several times if I was absolutely positive I wanted to go through with it. 'This is permanent,' she said. As if I couldn't grasp the concept. After I convinced Counselor Brandy that I was at least partially sane, Bonnie B. brought me to another waiting room. *9 to 5*, that Dolly Parton movie, was on but no one seemed to be watching it. And no one said anything. Some women stared off into space with tears threatening to fall, others bit their nails and tapped their feet, and the remaining women angrily flipped through out dated magazines.

Finally Bonnie B. led me into a surgical room which looked just like any other gynecologist office only with more medical equipment. I was allowed to keep my socks, bra and sweatshirt on. The elderly doctor kept urging me to shimmy my backside lower, just like Dr. Stevens does. I wish I could say it hurt like hell, but it didn't. I just laid there and stared at the ceiling, and tried not to think about what the whirring sound meant.

After the procedure, which took like five minutes, Bonnie B. led me to a recovery room, which was bare except for a few chairs and a table. She handed me a light sedative, enormous maxi pads, apple juice and peanut butter crackers. Bonnie B. strongly suggested I use birth control from then on and ordered that I make an appointment with my gynecologist within a few days. After about twenty minutes, I was free to leave the clinic. And that was it."

"Wow. How do you feel? I mean emotionally?" I ask.

"I hate to admit this even to you but I feel relieved. As if this was an inconvenience; like a cavity."

"Mom and Pete would have raised it, or some other couple would have."

"Chloe, are you trying to make me feel worse? Don't you think I know you're the good twin?"

"I'm sorry but for once I don't know what to say or do to make you feel better."

"I think the only thing that will make me feel better is time. What a cliché."

Corinne goes on to explain she had been two months along and the baby had weighed about an ounce, had started to develop a head, eyes, mouth, legs, arms, and organs including a heart and lungs. For some reason I think it was a boy.

We talk until Pete bangs on the door and tells me to "get off the phone and go to bed." Obviously Pete and Mom are ignoring Corinne for what she did.

I went to sleep that night thinking Corinne's relief might one day grow into sadness, guilt, and regret. Although my sister and I are nineteen-years-old and technically adults; it's as if we're in limbo with half of our bodies stuck in childhood and half in adulthood. Corinne fell asleep clutching the stuffed reindeer.

At ten o'clock the next morning I find a message on my cell phone. "Chloe, this is Bonnie B. from the clinic. We just want to make sure you are fine and well. Please give us a call back at 443-391-0054."

"I'm fine." I whisper while waking up alone in my twin bed clutching a stuffed reindeer.

***

"So what do you think?" I ask. It's a Saturday afternoon in mid February and my girlfriends and I are lounging in my bedroom.

"What happens next?" Liz wrinkles her small, pointed nose.

"Nothing; that was the end."

"But it doesn't feel complete," Celeste says.

"What do you mean?" I ask.

"First of all, I don't understand. What's wrong with Chloe? Is she schizophrenic?" Celeste asks.

I light a Kool brand cigarette and rest my head against the wall. "Corrine is Chloe's alter ego."

"Oh, like Dr. Jekyll and Mr. Hyde," Liz says.

"Not really, because Chloe isn't all good and Corrine isn't all evil. No one is," I say.

"Then why did Corrine call Chloe 'the good twin?'" Liz asks.

"Chloe summons Corrine whenever she has to make a difficult decision." I close my eyes and exhale a ring of smoke.

"I think it would be more interesting if you talked about Jack more," Celeste says.

"Jack isn't supposed to be the focal point." I sigh.

"No offense, but if you're serious about becoming an author, you'll have to learn to accept criticism," Liz says.

"Why do some people think that adding 'no offense' to whatever insulting thing they say excuses their rudeness?" I ask.

"Easy girls. Let's talk about something else." Celeste places a Rusted Root CD into the player. Typically when I listen to their music- a percussion driven, eclectic mix of African, Latin American, and Native American beats- I dance around with a huge grin on my face. But I don't feel like dancing right now.

"What's your view on abortion?" Liz stares at me.

"I don't think that it's all right or all wrong. It's one of those issues that fall into the gray area."

"It's pretty clear to me considering its murder." Liz's cheeks flush.

"It's also considered a medical procedure," I say.

"So what concert are we going to next?" Celeste asks.

"It's wrong, period," Liz says.

"I wouldn't make absolute statements until I've walked in another person's purple Doc Martens," I say.

"It's different when it's morally wrong," Liz says.

"Get. Out. Of. My. House." I feel my nostrils flare and my left fist clench.

Liz's mouth drops open as she grabs her hemp purse. Like Tinkerbelle, she flits down the steps before slamming the front door.

"What was that all about?" Celeste asks. She inches closer to me and strokes my hair.

"I can't stand judgmental people, especially when they're supposed to be my friends."

"Is there something else you want to tell me, Talia?" Celeste asks.

"No. I'm fine."

***

I often feel like a well-worn 3x3x3 Rubik's cube with peeling, fading stickers. Perhaps Corrine is the top level, Chloe the bottom, and whatever left of Talia in the center.

In real life, the ass's name isn't Jack and he's not my boyfriend. His actual name is Mark and he's my uncle. He's married to my Aunt Sherrie, who is my mother's youngest sister. Like Uncle Ted, the character in my story, Mark is an auction junkie and borderline hoarder. He's also the one who insisted I abort the pregnancy.

Mark began to pluck the feathers off my innocence six years ago, when I was thirteen and he was twenty- one. It was Easter Sunday and the entire family was gathered at Grandma and Pap's. Half were eating dinner on the sun porch and the rest at the dining room table, including me. My eight-year-old cousin

Alexia sat to my left and my thirty-some-year-old Uncle Don sat to my right. I was spooning potato salad onto my plate when Aunt Sherrie entered the room.

"Mark, this is everyone, everyone, this is Mark." She giggled. Aunt Sherrie and a god of some sort sat in the chairs across from me.

The first things I noticed were his full lips and straight white teeth. Then I admired his five o'clock shadow, prominent nose, wavy black hair, and his piercing green eyes…which at some point met mine.

I had felt tingles between my thighs before, but these tingles were like the Grand Finale of a Fourth of July fireworks exhibition.

With Mark at the table, dinner was both excruciating and fascinating. I divided the time between fantasizing about touching Mark's body and comparing my body to my aunt's. Her round, full breasts were like cantaloupes whereas mine were barely plums. She was thick, voluptuous. My body was trim yet muscular from years of ballet class. Her facial features were soft and pretty but so were mine. However, she smiled so easily, whereas my lips were typically pursed in a frown. Once my favorite aunt, Sherrie was now my competition.

***

Several Sundays later, my mother asked if I would bring her a Diet Coke from the fridge in the basement. Reluctantly, I ambled down the rickety steps. Mark was making a cocktail behind the bar.

"Hi, Mark." Grinning, I slid onto a bar stool.

"What'll it be?"

"Just a Diet Coke for my mother, please."

"And what would you like?" He smirked.

"I guess a Sprite."

"Nah, I'll make you a Screw Driver instead."

"What's that?" I wrinkled my nose.

"It's just vodka and orange juice."

"Then why is it called a Screw Driver?"

"In the 1950's, American engineers working in the Middle East oil fields would mix vodka into small cans of orange juice and mix it with a screw driver."

"Oh." While he mixed the cocktail, I noticed a tattoo underneath the right side of his white tee shirt. "I didn't know you had a tattoo."

He pulled up the sleeve of his shirt, exposing a black dragon. "You can touch it if you want."

I reached across the bar and gingerly touched his tattoo while my heart raced and chills traveled through my body. He tilted my face towards his, as if he were about to kiss me, however, he abruptly let go when my cousin Matt bounded down the steps.

"Enjoy the orange juice." He winked as I backed out of the basement clutching my cocktail and my mother's Diet Coke.

"What'll it be, Matt?"

***

I grew bolder as the months passed. Once I followed Mark upstairs and waited for him outside the bathroom. When he emerged, I took his hand and led him into a guest bedroom, which my mother and Aunt Sherrie used to share.

"What do you think you're doing?" He whispered as we fell side by side onto the bed.

"I just want to talk."

"About what?" He fingered my lips before cupping my chin.

"Do you think I'm pretty?"

"Dangerously so." He crushed his lips against mine.

His hands slipped beneath my blouse and hovered against my bra. "We can't do this, Talia."

"Why not?"

"You know why. Pretend this never happened." He stood and walked swiftly toward the door without a backward glance.

***

After that encounter, my goal was to tease and tempt him whenever possible, which was much easier in the summer months when I could parade around in a bikini. However, the summer I turned sixteen was the worst summer of my young life because that summer Mark proposed to Sherrie. They married the following spring and I spent the majority of the time throwing up in the church restroom. At the reception, I drank watered down Screw Drivers and remained in the shadows of their wedded bliss.

***

Late that night, I gathered every birthday and Christmas gift Mark had ever given me: a small box to house trinkets, a red journal made of pleather, a green cubic zirconia ring, a faux silver plated writing pen, a stuffed swan wearing a ballet costume, a pink locker mirror, bangle bracelets and a black beaded purse. I wanted to destroy all of it but when I picked up the stuffed swan, all I could do was cry.

***

Less than a year later, Aunt Sherrie gave birth to a daughter. Without consulting with me, my mother said that I would be more than happy to watch Hannah whenever they needed some alone time, which turned out to be that summer.

Mark insisted on picking me up, so I reluctantly climbed into his new red truck. I wish I could say that I felt no butterflies but they were fluttering throughout my entire body.

"Hi, Talia." He grinned.

"Hi. Do you mind if I smoke?"

"Sorry, no smoking in the new truck."

I shoved the cigarette packet into my purse.

"I have Altoids if you want." He fished in the middle compartment until he found a tin.

"Thanks, but I hate cinnamon."

He nodded and fiddled with the stereo. "Strawberry Wine" blared from the speakers and he sang along.

I couldn't help but laugh. "So Aunt Sherrie has brainwashed you into liking country, huh?"

"It's not half bad," he said.

"Who sings this song?"

"Deana Carter."

"Let's keep it that way," I said.

He reached over and played with the threads hanging from my jean short cutoffs, before his fingers traveled higher. I closed my eyes and rested my head against the leather upholstery.

"Let's take a detour," he said. His voice sounded thick like syrup. At the next street he turned right which led to the local make out spot. After he parked, he pulled down my shorts. I didn't stop him.

***

Like clockwork, with each passing birthday and Christmas I received another gift from Mark: strawberry scented body spray, a jewelry box with a plastic ballerina, Altoid tins in every flavor but cinnamon, fluffy pink slippers, earrings which left green marks on my ear lobes, and lastly the stuffed reindeer.

***

The night of the abortion, I gathered all the gifts and shoved them into a black garbage bag. After I was certain that my mother and stepfather were asleep, I crept into my white Pontiac Sunfire and drove to the local make out spot. I built a pyramid of gifts in the center of a fire pit and lit a match. I saved the stuffed reindeer for the grand finale.

EVEN IN DEATH

A Flower Story

Hunched over her late mother's arts and crafts table, sixty-seven-year-old Julie Plant clutches a green crayon and sticks her tongue between her thin lips. "How many more leaves should I add to this daisy?"

Big Orange Kitty nudges her foot with his head. "Not now, B.O.K., Mama's busy. You'll get your treats in a minute." She glances at the owl shaped kitchen timer. "Yep, in exactly one minute." She quickly adds another leaf to the flower drawing before the timer buzzes. "Two o'clock, now it's time for treats." B.O.K. trails her into the galley kitchen. As Julie struggles to open the fish flavored treat bag, he meows.

"I know what you're thinking. Slow as molasses-asses, mama. Meow, meow, meow. Hurry up with those treats. Slow as molasses-asses, mama," Julie trills. Her mother used to say that's what B.O.K. was thinking whenever she took too long to dish out his treats. Julie found it funny, and still does, but she knows that B.O.K. would never cuss, even in his thoughts. Julie counts out seven treats, not ten but seven, because that's how many Dr. Vet said B.O.K. was allowed each day. "Did it hurt your feelings when Dr. Vet said you have marmalade colored love handles?" She drops the treats in front of him. He chews loudly.

She peeks at the kitchen calendar. "You just had your checkup last week, so we don't get to see Dr. Vet for a long time." She sticks out her bottom lip but quickly pulls it back when she remembers what her mother used to say. "Julie, a bird's going to poop on that lip if you're not careful."

Meow.

"Sorry kitty, but no more."

Last week she explained to Dr. Vet, "But food makes him happy, like flowers make me happy. I love him and want him to be happy."

"I know how much you care for him, Julie." He placed a hand on her shoulder and gave it a light squeeze. "Most cats stop eating when they're full but B.O.K. is like a goldfish; he eats and eats until eventually he'll explode."

Julie took a huge breath and held it. Her thin cheeks expanded like a puffer fish. After a few seconds she exhaled. "Will he explode like that?"

"Just like that." Dr. Vet bit his bottom lip to keep from laughing.

"How long do you think I held my breath? At least two minutes, right?" Julie asked.

"Almost." Dr. Vet couldn't help but smile.

Thinking about Dr. Vet made Julie giggle. He was as handsome as the men on the soap operas. His hair and mustache were the color of salt and pepper. He graduated a few years ahead of her and like her, never married. She wished he would have asked her on a date and brought her pink orchids. Maybe she should ask Dr. Vet to go to the aquarium with her. But then she remembered what her mother used to say: "Good girls don't ask boys on dates and most boys don't bring flowers. And if they do, they expect to rub their stamen against your carpel." Julie didn't want anyone to fondle any part of her pink flower; she just wanted to watch the sea turtles swim in the large tank.

"I'll just draw a picture of the sea turtles surrounded by flowers." She bobs her head and rubs her hands together. "But first, it's nap time." She crawls on the pea green couch and snuggles under a rainbow colored afghan. B.O.K. nestles on her chest and stretches out his paws, lightly scratching her chin. Within minutes their breathing patterns match. 'What a long day' is Julie's last thought before she succumbs to sleep.

A FLOWER STORY

For Julie, every day resembles the movie *Groundhog Day*, where an obnoxious weather man covering the event finds himself repeating the same day over and over, but Julie is content with the same old, same old.

Sylvia Bitters parks her Cadillac DeVille directly in front of Julie's house. She pats the dashboard. "You did good, old girl." Her husband and son consistently hound her to buy a newer car but her caddy has been good to her all these years. And it wasn't like either of them have the money to buy her a fancier vehicle, unless it's the size of a Matchbox car. She imagines Carl, her husband of twenty-five years, offering her a miniature car wrapped in a little bow. His pudgy hands would be sweaty and warm, his smile wavering between apprehension and excitement. "Pathetic," she snorts.

She lifts two grocery bags from the trunk before waddling up the front steps. As soon as Sylvia enters the hallway, she hears Julie and the "pain in the ass" cat snoring.

"Must be nice to snooze in the middle of the day," she mutters. She makes sure to make a racket putting the peanut butter, vegetable soup and tuna fish cans in the kitchen cupboard. Then she half-heartedly wipes the counter tops, empties the dishwasher, and replaces the hand soap. Time for a break.

She picks up several paper flowers from the recliner as if they were her husband Carl's stinky tighty whities. "It's like that freaking V.C. Andrews' novel *Flowers in the Attic* up in here, where those captive children create a paper flower gar den in the attic. Wish I had time for that crap. What time is it anyway?" She glances at the clock; five until three, just in time for *Family Feud* reruns. She plops into the recliner and turns on the TV.

"Hi, Sylvia," Julie says, stretching her arms over her head and yawning. "Can we watch *Days of Our Lives* now?"

"Nah, I don't like that fantasy crap with all those plastic people. You recorded it, right? Watch it later."

"Sure, I can watch it later. I'll draw instead." Before she died, Julie's mother taught her how to record shows using the VCR. Julie missed the way her mother smelled, (like citronella candles and talcum powder) the way she cooked, (especially lasagna with pepperoni and green peppers) and most of all, she missed how much her mother loved her.

Growing up, Julie did a lot of bad things but she did them because kids were so cruel to her. In second grade, Julie cut a chunk of Melissa's hair off for calling her a 'retard.' That afternoon, Melissa's mother took her to a stylist who cut her hair so short she looked like a boy. Melissa's new nickname was Marvin.

In fifth grade Tommy told her she should be riding the short bus and the entire class laughed. At recess during Valentine's Day, Julie got even by licking all of the lollipops Tommy brought. She rubbed them against her sweater before rewrapping each one. Olivia, the girl Tommy liked, was the first to discover the disgusting pops.

"Eww, Tommy, there's fur on this one and it's sticky."

Tommy's face turned bright red. "I'm sorry, Olivia. Here's a new one."

Olivia frowned while she inspected another lollipop. "There's fur on this one, too."

Tommy's new nickname was Fuzz.

Each time Julie did something naughty, she'd ask her mother, "Do you still love me?"

And her mother would answer, "Julie Plant, I will love you even after we become plant food." The memory makes Julie giggle.

"What's so funny? You're so weird, Julie, do you know that? Don't bother answering, my show's back on," Sylvia says.

"And you're the biggest bully of all," Julie says under her breath. Sylvia has been Julie's caretaker for a month now and it's time for her to move on.

Julie slips out the front door while Sylvia yells at the TV. "Come on Wilson family, the number one item families run out of each week has got to be toilet paper. Not bologna. Not spaghetti. And not juice. It's TP!"

Since Julie's father took off for Reno shortly after she was born, her mother had to learn how to do everything on her own, including taking care of their vehicle. Even though Julie couldn't drive due to her special-ness, her mother insisted that she learn about vehicles. "It's important to be a well-rounded person, Julie," she said.

"What should I do to the witch's car?" Julie sticks her tongue between her lips and wanders around the garage. A rusty gas can catches her eye. She unscrews the lid and takes a tentative whiff. Her eyes immediately water and she coughs. "The only thing pleasant about diesel is that it causes witches cars and broom sticks to stall," she says. She pours a gallon of diesel into the Cadillac's tank. Then she returns to the living room.

After *Family Feud*, Sylvia reluctantly rises from the recliner. "I have to go cook for Carl and Charlie now. I bought some of those frozen meatloaf dinners you like so much, maybe you can eat one of those. Or make a tuna sandwich but don't give any to that fat cat. I'll see you tomorrow."

"Bye," Julie says, looking out the living room window as Sylvia shuffles down the steps. Then Sylvia climbs into her caddy and turns the key several times. A minute later, she scrambles out of the car, slowly ascends the front steps, and enters the house.

"I can't believe my bad luck. My caddy won't start," she says. Julie places her hand over her mouth to hide her smile. Using Julie's rotary phone, Sylvia dials Carl at work but his secretary says he's left for the day. Next she calls home but no one answers. As a last resort, she punches in Charlie's number.

"Yellow," Charlie says.

"How many times do I have to tell you, 'hello' is a greeting, 'yellow' is a color? Regardless, my car won't start. You'll have to pick me up at 88 Mulberry Lane."

"But I'm working, maw. And I'm nowhere near there."

"The only work you accomplish is getting stoned. I don't know why Mr. Moss hasn't fired you yet."

"It's for medicinal purposes, maw, you know that. Just look how clear my skin is. And I really am busy, you know, working."

"Selling pot out of an elderly man's flower truck is disgraceful."

Charlie continues to whine but Sylvia stops listening. She barks, "Tough doo-doo. Come and get me." After she hangs up the phone, she turns to Julie. "Will you be a dear and wait for my son Charlie to come? He drives a green Dodge Neon." Without waiting for a response, she collapses into the recliner.

"Come on, B.O.K." Julie and her cat curl up on the front porch swing. "Let's pretend Dr. Vet is my beau and he's taking me to a fancy restaurant with tablecloths and waiters and waitresses. And surely he'll bring flowers, but what kind? Maybe carnations, those are crinkly like tissue paper, and I like them. After dinner, I'll beg him to take me to the aquarium to see the sea turtles." She rocks so quickly on the wooden swing, it's a wonder B.O.K. doesn't throw up the fish flavored treats.

Approximately twenty minutes later, the sound of tires crunching gravel shakes her from her reverie. Could it be Dr. Vet? Or is it just Sylvia's son? When she realizes it's a flower delivery truck, she leaps from the swing, and B.O.K. sails through the air, limbs outstretched like a ninja.

"Oh my stars, real flowers from Dr. Vet to me, Julie Plant." She scurries down the steps as quickly as her old limbs allow. At the end of the driveway, she bounces like a Mexican jumping bean soaked in espresso.

Meanwhile in the flower truck, Charlie drops a lit joint on his naked foot.

"Crap." He bends to retrieve it. While feeling under the seat, he discovers a significantly large bag of weed. "So this is where it went." In a moment of potted bliss, he mistakes the gas pedal for the brakes.

As the flower truck careens toward her, Julie's mouth opens but no words come out. After the accident, plenty of words fly out of Charlie's mouth, especially when the police arrive to arrest him.

Three days later, Julie is laid to rest. Dr. Vet is the only person besides the minister in attendance. B.O.K. meows pitifully from the cat carrier. Dr. Vet places a bouquet of long-stem pink roses on Julie's chest. "Don't worry Julie, I'll take care of B.O.K. I wish I would have given you flowers while you were still alive to smell them."

Loose Ends

Present, Wednesday, June 26, 2013

Kitty Anthony stares at her shrink's Swarovski stilettos, transfixed by their bling.

"What are you thinking about, Kitty?" Dr. Morgan says.

"I wore similar shoes that night but mine were knockoffs. I left them on the lawn after a guy puked on them."

Dr. Morgan tilts her head. "Are you ready to tell me the whole story?" Since Kitty started counseling last autumn, she had disclosed bits and pieces of what happened that night, but she was afraid to reveal everything because if she did, certainly Dr. Morgan would have her committed to a psych ward. And yet, Kitty feels compelled to tell her story, or more aptly, Layla's story.

Kitty nods slowly, as if she were slipped a roofie. "I think so."

Dr. Morgan leans forward and clasps her hands. "Why don't you start from the beginning?"

Kitty runs her nails across her strawberry blonde scalp, resisting the urge to yank out a strand. She suffers from trichotillomania, a hair pulling disorder, along with generalized anxiety, and post traumatic stress disorder; all caused by a decision she made over a year ago, on the night of Rachel Riley's party.

Kitty slips her hands under her thighs, because once she starts talking about that night, the obsessive-compulsive hair pulling cycle will surely start. "It sounds stupid now but I was so excited that day. The look on my brother's face when he entered my room was priceless…"

Past, Friday, June 15, 2012

"It looks like the Wet Seal threw up in here." James said in reference to the dresses, jeans, tops, shoes, jewelry, and makeup that covered every inch of Kitty's bedroom.

She laughed. "I actually did buy some dresses from that store."

He crinkled his nose. "What's all this for?"

"For Rachel Riley's party. Don't tell me you forgot. James, you promised."

He flipped his sandy blonde hair and sighed. "You owe me big time."

"It can count as my birthday present."

"It means that much to you?"

"Yes. This party is going to be off the hook."

"Since when do you use expressions like that? And since when do you care about Rachel Riley? She's just a snotty-biatch."

"Doesn't matter. It's the last hoorah of our senior year and everyone who attends Rachel's parties say they're the best. Granted, I only received the invite because I promised you'd attend, but regardless, I got the invite. Now, I just have to decide on the perfect outfit." She picked up a turquoise sun dress and spun around.

James rolled his eyes. "Who gave you a lobotomy? You sound like one of those chicks from the *Mean Girls* movie."

"I'll go back to being boring old Katherine tomorrow, I promise."

"You better. See you later, squirt." He walked toward the door.

"What time will you be there?"

"Whenever the 'rents relive me. You owe me for taking your shift, too. My buddies are headed to the *Prometheus* premier, and you know how much of a sci-fi geek I am."

"You're the best brother, like ever." Kitty flung her arms around James' waist and squeezed him like a peach.

At seven o'clock, as Kitty stepped into the shower, her cell phone rang. She grabbed it off of the sink and groaned when the screen flashed "Pam." She hopped from one foot to the other, debating whether or not to answer the call. If she didn't answer, her mother would keep calling and leaving messages until she did.

"Hi, Mom."

"Kitty, we're buried. Can you please work for a few hours? A customer spilled a bowl of cheddar broccoli soup on Geraldine's arm. It looked like a first degree burn but we erred on the side of caution and sent her to the hospital."

"But, Mom, tonight's Rachel's party and I hardly ever request a night off."

"I know sweetheart but we really need you. And we'll get you out as soon as possible, by nine?"

"I'll be there in fifteen minutes."

"Thanks so much. See you soon."

Kitty dressed in jeans, a green work shirt and matching apron, and pulled her hair into a pony tail. In her '98 Honda Civic, Kitty blasted "You Can't Always Get What You Want" by the Rolling Stones. Fortunately, The Gingerbread Man, her family's restaurant, which most people referred to as 'The G-Man,' was only a mile from their home. She parked next to her parent's minivan.

As soon as she walked through the door, she regretted answering her mother's phone call because the G-Man was beyond slammed. As usual, her mother's hair was in a messy ponytail, her shirt was stained with either ketchup or marinara sauce, and the expression on her face shouted "Calgon, take me the hell away from here!" James on the other hand, looked like he just stepped off an Abercrombie and Fitch runway but he was modeling khaki shorts and the G-Man tee.

"Kitty, you're on section three. Orders should be up." Her mother shouted over the noise from the jukebox and patrons.

Kitty hesitated before opening the kitchen door. Her father was the head chef and by this point, a blood vessel most likely had popped in one or both of his eyes. Off the clock her father had a Type B personality, at work not so much.

"It's best to get it over with," James said, pushing past her into the kitchen. She followed suit. James handed an oversized tray to her and loaded it with plates of fish and chips, burgers, and hot wings. "Table 12. Push the blackened salmon."

"On it, boss."

Before she left the kitchen, she took a quick look at her father. His face resembled a sweaty, ripe tomato. She would skip the hello.

Even though the next hour and a half passed quickly, Kitty found the time to glance at the clock every fifteen minutes. She made a mental list of all of the things that she had to do after work: take a shower, defrizz her hair, carefully apply her new makeup, and pick out an outfit...Maybe Alex Vincent would notice her tonight.

"Excuse me." A girl with short red hair waved a placard in Kitty's face. "It says here that you'll drive someone home if they're drunk?"

Kitty fought the urge to roll her eyes. "Yes, we participate in the designated driver program."

The red head squinted at Kitty. "So you'll drive us home?" Her friends resembled the *Sweet Valley High* twins.

"As long as it's within a fifteen minute radius."

"It is." The blonde wearing violet lipstick said with a hiccup.

"Hey, Mom," Kitty called across the restaurant. She held up three fingers to represent section three, pointed to the girls, and pretended like she was driving a car.

Her mother nodded.

The three girls followed Kitty to the parking lot.

"Hop in." Kitty opened her car door and pushed the seat up so the twins could crawl in the backseat.

"Why can't we get a ride in this?" The blonde wearing mauve lipstick pressed against James' '68 Dodge Charger. James never let anyone drive his car. Plus the rule was, Kitty drove female patrons home, James drove male patrons.

"I can always call you a cab," Kitty said.

"We're fine." The red head pushed her friends in the backseat before collapsing in the passenger seat.

"Where to?" Kitty said.

"Bennington. By the way, I'm Tamara."

"I'm Kitty." Ironically, Rachel Riley lived in the same development. Kitty made a right turn out of the parking lot and headed east.

"Will my car be ticketed or like towed? And how come the G-Man offers free rides?" Violet lips said.

"Your car will be fine overnight but please pick it up tomorrow. Two years ago my cousin Chris was killed by a drunk driver. My family decided to participate in this program to save other people's lives."

"How incredibly depressing." Tamara said. "Mind if I turn the radio on?"

Kitty shook her head. She was forced to listen to Justin Beiber and other teeny bopper music the entire way to Bennington.

"It's the white house with the black shutters," Tamara pointed out the window.

After the girls climbed out of her car, Kitty signed with relief. She watched as they kicked their heels off and ran through the grass. Mauve lips attempted a cart wheel. Kitty couldn't remember the last time she did anything solely for fun. She was always working, studying, and preparing for college. Maybe tonight would be different, or even magical.

Back at the G-Man, Kitty surveyed the crowd; hectic but more manageable than two hours prior. Her mother was leaning against the bar, waiting for drinks. Kitty made her way across the restaurant.

"Mom, how's it going?"

Pam brushed her bangs across her forehead. "Is it margarita o'clock yet? Thanks for your help, sweetie. I hope you have a blast at the party."

"Thanks. I'd hug you but I guarantee we're both stinky."

Pam laughed. "I hope you're taking a shower first."

"For the party of the century, why bother? See you later, love you."

"Not too late, you're not eighteen yet. Love you, too."

Kitty spotted James at the register.

"Don't forget to come, okay? Even if it's for a few minutes. Rachel Riley will freak if you don't show," she said.

"Relax squirt. If I were you, I'd get out now while the going is good."

"Good idea. Bye, James."

"Bye."

Before Kitty made it to the exit, a tall brunette motioned to her. "You work here, right?"

Reluctantly, Kitty nodded.

"My boyfriend and I were arguing before he up and left. He's done this before but he's always come back. However, I don't think he's coming back this time. I've had too much to drink and this placard mentions a program where employees drive patrons home for free."

Kitty checked her watch: nine-fifteen. "Where do you live?" she asked.

"Mayberry."

Inwardly, Kitty cringed. The Mayberry Development was practically in the next town. At this rate she'd never get to the party.

"I'm really sorry but I'm off the clock. Should I call you a cab?"

The brunette shook her head. "I should be okay. I'll just stay a bit longer and drink some water. Randy drove off in his friend's truck, so I can drive my car home."

Kitty felt a twinge of guilt but pushed it away. Besides, compared to the other three girls, this girl appeared perfectly sober.

Kitty nodded. "Bye."

"Have a good night," she said.

On the way home, Kitty sang along to one of Janis Joplin's greatest hits, "Try" (Just a Little Bit Harder). The song reminded her of Alex Vincent, who she had a crush on since the forth grade. This year they finally landed in the same art class and both were quite talented. Kitty focused on painting and Alex was a sculptor. However, Kitty found it hard to concentrate on her canvas when Alex was so close. He was uncharacteristically handsome with dark, close set eyes, shaggy black hair, a muscular but thin frame, and he smelled damp and musty, just like the clay pressed between his fingers. Kitty had an inkling that he liked her because he often complimented her paintings and said hello to her at the start of class.

It was nine-forty before Kitty stepped into the shower. She scrubbed the scents from the G-Man including smoke, grease, and ranch dressing off her skin and hair. Twenty minutes later, she smelled like a coconut, her favorite fruit. After blow drying and straightening her hair, Kitty painted her face as carefully as she would a canvas. Then she shimmied into a strapless red dress. She finished the look with minimal jewelry and silver stilettos.

On her way to Rachel's party, her heart beat erratically. It was after eleven o'clock by the time she arrived. She reapplied reddish orange lipstick and fluffed her hair before she climbed out of her car. She felt like an outcast in a Lifetime movie. Fortunately, a group of kids from her calculus class were hanging out in the kitchen, so she joined them.

"Is that you, Kitty? Me-ow." David eyed her up and down.

"You sure clean up well," Ed said.

Kitty blushed until her cheeks matched her dress.

"Maybe you should go outside with the other male chauvinistic pigs," Morgan said to David and Ed. She stuck out her tongue and pushed up her nose.

"Is Alex Vincent out there?" Kitty said.

"Haven't seen him. Have a drink." Morgan handed Kitty a Miller Lite beer and she pretended to take a sip. Kitty didn't like the taste of or the side effects from alcohol, so at one point she would dump it.

Rachel waltzed into the kitchen, wearing a dress you would find at a bridal store. Her hair was pulled back in a modern chignon. When she spotted Kitty, her dark eyes narrowed. "Where's James?"

Kitty checked her cell phone for the time. "He should be here any minute."

"Send him my way as soon as he arrives. I'll be on the deck." She turned to David and Ed. "Boys, can you please bring another keg out back?"

When Rachel was out of earshot, Morgan said, "Is she marrying your brother tonight?"

Kitty giggled. "Oh, hell no."

Morgan looped her arm through Kitty's. "Let's go mingle."

Outside, most of their classmates were playing alcohol related games such as beer pong, corn hole, and keg stands. Kitty surveyed the crowd but didn't spot Alex. Instead, Rachel's eyes bore into her.

"Which game do you want to play? Looks like David and Ed are in line for corn hole," Morgan said.

"Actually, I have to use the restroom. I'll be right back." What she needed to do was escape Rachel's probing eyes. Kitty entered the house and walked into the kitchen. There was no one around, so she dumped her beer down the drain. Then she grabbed a bottled water from the fridge.

"Now how many waters have you consumed tonight, miss? No more than one per hour, I hope." James said.

"I'm so glad you're here. I'm pretty sure Rachel was about to kick me out."

"Well, you're safe now. Where is she? I want to get this over with because I am tired as all get out. After my shower, I was ready for lights out." James shook damp hair from his eyes.

Kitty handed him a Red Bull. "This will wake you up. Let's join the party."

As soon as James stepped onto the deck, Rachel tackled him like a seagull would attack boardwalk fries. In fact, in her white dress, scrawny legs, and screeching voice, Rachel could pass as a seagull.

Feeling bad for her brother, Kitty joined Morgan and the boys at the corn hole game.

"Hey isn't that Alex doing a keg stand?" Morgan said.

Kitty peered into the darkness. "I think it is. Here goes nothing." With her head held high, she sauntered across the lawn and stood in front of him. Alex wiped beer from his chin and throat with a towel.

Instead of saying hello, Kitty simply stared.

"Kitty, are you okay? You look like you've seen a ghost."

"No, I'm fine. I think I just had too much to drink," she lied.

"Well let me know if you need a ride home."

A thrill ran up and down Kitty's spine. "That would be fantastic."

"Great, I'll let you know when Sadie and I are leaving."

"Sadie?" Kitty frowned.

"Sadie Rivers. We've been dating for a few weeks now."

Kitty's hope diminished like the sun behind a massive cloud.

Alex clutched his stomach. Before Kitty realized what was happening, he vomited all over her knock off stilettos.

"I'm so sorry." Alex attempted to clean off her shoes using the beer towel.

"Don't be, they were cheap." Kitty stepped out of them. The grass beneath her feet felt surprisingly cool. James and Rachel were sharing an Adirondack chair. Before Kitty had the chance to tell James he was off the hook, he cupped Rachel's face and kissed her.

"Can this night get any worse?" Kitty mumbled as she walked out the front door.

The next morning, Kitty felt bitter. She contemplated returning all of her purchases but decided she was feeling too lazy and depressed to face the mall crowd. Instead, she spent the day in bed with a carton of Neapolitan ice cream and a horror novel.

At one point, James checked in on her. "I'm sorry about Alex and your shoes."

"How did you know I liked Alex?"

James grinned. "I think *everyone* knows that you've been crushing on him since like middle school."

Kitty groaned. "More like fourth grade. I don't want to talk about it. So I saw you kissing Rachel. What was that all about?"

"We actually hit it off. Don't be mad squirt, but I'm taking her to the movies tonight."

Kitty placed a throw pillow against her face and screamed.

That evening, she went through the motions at work. All she could think about was Alex and Sadie Rivers. Sadie wasn't particularly smart or cute. She must be funny, Kitty decided.

Granted, her heart was temporarily wounded but in the fall when she moved to Pittsburgh to attend The School of Art at Carnegie Mellon, she would have so many guys after her that she would have to fight them off with a soaked paintbrush. She laughed at her lame fantasy.

At eleven-thirty, two inebriated girls trailed Kitty through the parking lot. Their faces had a green tint to them and the girl with dark hair clutched her stomach.

"I'm never doing a Jagerbomb again," she wailed.

Kitty rooted through the glove compartment and pulled out plastic bags.

"If you're going to be sick, please use these." Kitty handed them each a bag.

At the first red light, Kitty glanced into her rear view mirror. One of the girls rested her head against the window as the other heaved into a bag. Clearly Brad served them way too many drinks. He had been warned about over serving before. Kitty made a mental note to speak to her parents about him. In the meantime, she rolled down her window. She also sprayed a healthy dose of white vinegar inside the car.

"You don't get paid enough for this shit, Kitty-cat," one of the girls said.

"Can you tell my parents that? By the way how did you know my father's nickname for me?"

"What?" One of the girls said.

"I said, can you tell my parents that?"

"I don't know what you're talking about," she said.

Had someone slipped a roofie into her iced tea? Kitty smacked her cheeks a few times to snap out of it.

"How was your party, Kitty-cat?"

Kitty glanced into her rearview mirror to find both girls resting.

"Who said that?" Kitty said.

"Why your passenger, silly."

Kitty looked to the right but saw nothing.

"Clearly I've been reading too many Steven King novels." She turned on the radio and sang along to the top forty hits until they arrived at the apartment complex. She pulled her car into a visitor spot.

"Wake up, girls," she said. They crawled from Kitty's car, leaving behind the smell of vomit and cigarette smoke.

"Get out of the car, Kitty-cat."

She clenched her eyes and leaned her forehead against the steering wheel.

"Kitty-cat, I told you to get out of the car."

Reluctantly, she opened her eyes and turned to find a female presence hovering over the passenger seat.

"What the f-"

"I'm Layla. Do you remember me?"

Kitty shook her head vigorously, like a dog after a dip in the lake. This must be a nightmare. Yes, that's all it was. She vowed to give up the horror genre; what she needed was romance in her life.

"I'm the girl from last night who drank too much. I asked for a ride home but you were off the clock. And no, this isn't a nightmare. Well, not yet, but if you don't get out of the f'ing car now, it might turn into one."

Kitty did as she was told.

"Aren't you going to ask what happened to me after I left the G-Man last night?"

"W-w-what happened?" Kitty stuttered.

"I drank another glass of water and then I got behind the wheel of my car. I realized that I wasn't sober after I drove through a Sheetz."

Kitty placed her hands on her face, resembling the man from Edvard Munch's painting, *The Scream*. "Oh my God. Was anyone else…hurt?"

"Fortunately, I was the only casualty."

"I think I'm going to be sick." Kitty sunk to the sidewalk and dropped her head between her knees. She took ten deep breaths before sitting up. "Are you blaming me for your accident?"

Layla cocked her head. "No, I'm not blaming you. I was the one who drank too many cocktails and I was the one who drove drunk."

"So what do you want from me?"

Layla floated next to Kitty. "I need your help. You see, I wasn't ready to die. You're probably thinking, is anyone ever ready to die? From my new perspective, I would say that some are more ready than others. Regardless, my friends and family weren't ready for me to die. Why don't people tell you how much you mean to them when you're still breathing?" Layla smiled but it resembled a fake, red carpet smile. "Do you know why there are spirits on Earth, Kitty-cat?"

When Kitty didn't respond, Layla continued.

"All the stuff they teach you during Sunday school is real; there is a Heaven and a Hell. However, before a spirit is welcome to either place, they must tie up their loose ends on Earth. That's where you come in. I'd explain it all now but it looks like you've heard enough for one night, so I'll visit tomorrow. Ciao." Layla's spirit disappeared.

Kitty got back in her car and drove home. "People hallucinate when they're exhausted and that's what's happening to me." She repeated this phrase several times.

Unfortunately when she woke up the next morning, Layla was perched on her window seat. "You snore like really loud," she said.

Kitty groaned.

"Wake up, Kitty-cat; we have a busy day ahead of us."

Kitty took a quick shower, dressed in jeans and a tee shirt, and followed Layla outside. As long as Layla didn't ask her to break the law, she'd help her. The sooner Layla was out of her life, the better.

Layla pouted. "I can read your thoughts you know."

Kitty had the urge to yank Layla's hair. Since this was impossible, she pulled out a few strands of her own, which was strangely satisfying. Maybe she was caffeine deprived. Yes, coffee would definitely help.

"It's too early for a cat fight, Kitty-cat. And our first stop is at the Sheetz near Mayberry and their coffee isn't half bad," Layla said.

Kitty's eyes grew wide. "The Sheetz that you drove into?"

"No, silly, there are two near my house. The one on Washington is most likely closed for repairs. I bet their employees are thanking me right now. Paid time off!"

"How can you joke about...dying?" Kitty said.

Layla shrugged. "What's the alternative?"

Kitty drove to the Sheetz on Lincoln Avenue and parked.

"Order a sausage, egg, and cheese shmuffin. It's for my mom. Oh, and buy a can of shaving cream, the largest can they have," Layla said.

"Shaving cream? For what?" Kitty said.

"I'll tell you later."

After grabbing a can of shaving cream, Kitty ordered the sandwich and poured herself a jumbo size cup of coffee. Back in the car, Layla was singing along to "If I Die Young," by The Band Perry.

"Interesting choice," Kitty said.

"It fits," Layla said but she wasn't smiling.

They didn't talk until Kitty turned left into the Mayberry development.

"You're going to make another left on Hemlock Drive and my house is in the center of the cul-de-sac. You can park in the driveway."

Layla's house looked similar to Rachel's, and to all the other development homes. Kitty secretly preferred her older home with a yard larger than a postage stamp.

"I agree with you but for some reason, my parents love this house."

Kitty wiped her hands on her jeans. "What will I say?"

"Just say that we went to cosmetology school together."

"I don't want to lie to your mother."

"Would you rather tell her the truth?"

"Yes, I mean at least part of it. I can say that you and Randy hung out at the G-Man and that's how we got to know each other."

"That should work. I just want to check in on her," Layla said.

Holding the coffee and breakfast sandwich in one hand, Kitty rang the doorbell.

A moment later, a woman who could pass for Layla's sister opened the door. Her eyes were red rimmed and her face was splotchy from crying.

"Hi, I'm a friend of Layla's."

Layla's mother just stared at her.

"May I come in and talk to you for a minute?"

"Sure." She opened the door wider for Kitty to pass through. She followed Layla's mother into the kitchen.

"Please, have a seat. What's your name?"

"Kitty."

"My name is Veronica. It's nice to meet you. I'd offer you a cup of coffee but you have one."

"I brought this for you." Kitty handed the Sheetz bag to Veronica. "It's a shmuffin. Layla mentioned that was your favorite sandwich."

"She did? Her nickname for me is 'shmom.' She smiled through her tears. "What am I going to do without my Layla?"

Kitty reached across the table and held her hand. "I'm so sorry for your loss."

Layla perched on the chair next to her mother.

"So how did you and Layla know each other?"

"We met at my family's restaurant, The Gingerbread Man..."

Kitty and Veronica chatted for well over an hour before Kitty excused herself.

"It was so nice meeting you, please visit anytime." Veronica clasped Kitty's hands and smiled.

"I will."

Back in the car, Kitty said, "Where to next?"

"Downtown to Murray's Bookstore. By the way, thanks for being so nice to my mother. I just wanted to see her smile one more time."

Kitty nodded. She thought about how her mother would feel if the situations were reversed. She bit her lip to keep from crying.

Kitty parallel parked in front of the bookstore and waited for further instructions.

"My kid sister is a tougher nut to crack. She doesn't have many friends, keeps to herself, she's kind of awkward...you know, she's actually a lot like you."

"Wow, Layla, thanks. What am I supposed to say to your sister?"

"I want you to tell her that you're willing to help return all the things I stole."

"What?"

"I was a bit of a kleptomaniac and I stole a lot of things from various stores. The right thing to do is to return everything. Lauren will surely help you."

"How are we going to explain that?"

Layla shrugged. "I'm sure you'll think of something. Let's go." Layla left through the door without opening it. Very cool.

"I'd have to disagree with you on that. There's nothing cool about dying," Layla said.

"I'm sorry for thinking so insensitively." Kitty joined Layla on the sidewalk.

Layla smirked. "I'm just f'ing with you; the floating through shit is amazing."

When Kitty pushed the door to the bookstore, it wouldn't budge. She glanced at the sign. "It doesn't open for another ten minutes."

"Lauren's in there. Knock loudly and she'll eventually show."

Kitty did so and in less than a minute, Lauren opened the door a crack. She wasn't nearly as exotic looking as her sister and mother but she was cute with a slightly upturned nose, petite frame, and curly black hair.

"Can't you read?" She scowled.

"My name's Kitty. I'm a friend of your sister's."

Lauren's eyes narrowed. "Layla never mentioned you."

"Can I come in?"

After a beat, Lauren flung open the door. Kitty was hit with a musty scent mixed with olive oil. The bookstore was small but it was well-stocked and neat.

Lauren perched on a stool behind the counter. She motioned to the stool beside her and Kitty sat down. Layla hovered by the science fiction section.

"I'm surprised that you're here," Kitty said.

Lauren frowned. "Where else would I be?"

"I don't have much experience with losing a loved one but I assumed that people stayed home to mourn after a death? I'm sorry, I don't mean to pry."

"My boss said the same thing but I told him I'd much rather be here than at home with my mother, wallowing in self pity. My father went to work, too." She spent the next few minutes straightening the already organized counter, before she looked up at Kitty. "So how did you know my sister?"

In between customers, Kitty and Lauren talked about Layla. After half an hour, Kitty felt comfortable bringing up the subject she came to discuss.

"A few days ago Layla mentioned that she wanted to return the things she shoplifted."

Lauren's eyebrows rose. "She did?"

"Yes."

"Well, she can't do that now." She threw her hands up in the air.

"Maybe we can do it for her."

"But how would we know what was stolen?"

Kitty chewed her lip before coming up with the perfect lie. "She left me a list."

"Why would she do that?"

"Well, we were at the G-Man, and Randy was playing darts with his friends, and I was working, therefore, Layla was at the table alone."

Lauren snorted. "Sounds like Randy. What an a-hole."

"Layla was bored, so she grabbed a napkin and scribbled down all the things that she shoplifted. At least the recent things."

"Sounds like something my sister would do. But how is returning used shampoo bottles and miniskirts going to help anything?"

"I think it's what Layla would have wanted," Kitty said softly. "So will you help me?"

"How about tomorrow morning at ten o'clock? Can you pick me up at my house?"

"Sounds perfect."

Lauren grabbed a book mark and a pen. "Let me write down my address."

"No need, I know where you live."

Lauren cocked her head. "See you then."

"Bye."

Back in the safety of her car, Kitty sighed.

Layla laughed.

"What's so funny?"

"Did you see my sister's face after you said, 'I know where you live?' She probably thinks you're a stalker."

Kitty turned to Layla. "I'm doing the best I can."

"Relax, Kitty-cat, you did great. Now there's only one more stop and you're off the hook. After you help my sister tomorrow, of course."

Kitty groaned. "Now what?"

Layla rubbed her hands together. "Now we visit Randy."

"What am I going to say to him?"

"You're not going to say anything. I just want you to write a message on his car."

Kitty placed her hands on her hips. "No way. I'm not breaking the law."

"It's not breaking the law if you use shaving cream."

"No, I suppose it isn't. Alright, where to?"

"He actually lives near you. On Poplar Street."

Kitty took the next left and headed to Randy's house. Layla remained silent, staring out the window. The silence bothered Kitty, so she fiddled with the radio, stopping at a Depeche Mode song. As Poplar Street approached, Kitty slowed the car.

"There's his SUV." Layla pointed out the window. Fortunately, his car was parked on the street.

Kitty parked her car directly across the street. She snatched the can of shaving cream from the backseat and gave it a good shake. "What should I write?"

"I know what you did last summer, Randall."

"What does that mean?"

"A few months ago, I rented a horror movie called, *I Know What You Did Last Summer*, and for some reason, it really freaked him out. So late at night I would randomly whisper that in his ear, just to mess with him."

Kitty took a deep breath. "Time to get this over with." She sprang from the car. Before sprinting across, she looked up and down the street. She said a quick prayer that she wouldn't get caught, before she scribbled the message on Randy's vehicle. Then she darted back to her car.

"He's going to freak when he sees that!" Layla squealed.

"Can I go home now? I think I'm going to be sick," Kitty said.

"You'll be fine, just relax. Plus, we can't leave until we see Randy's reaction."

Kitty closed her eyes and slid as low as possible in her seat. "Just let me know when it's over." She was emotionally exhausted and immediately fell asleep. Sometime later, she woke to Layla whispering loudly in her ear.

"Wake up Kitty-cat, Randy and some bimbo are heading outside. He couldn't even wait until after my funeral to hook up. He really is an a-hole."

Kitty rubbed her eyes. "Maybe he doesn't know about your accident yet."

"Oh he knows alright. My sister called him. But none of that matters now."

Kitty peered out the window. Randy and a voluptuous blonde were holding hands. Kitty sank lower in her seat as they crossed the street. Randy shoved his tongue down the bimbo's throat before she climbed into her blue Toyota Camry, which was parked in front of Kitty's car. Randy watched as the blonde drove off, wearing a shit- eating grin.

"Wait for it," Layla whispered.

Randy strolled across the street but stopped abruptly when he noticed the message on his SUV. He wailed, "Layla," just like Sylvester Stallone shouted Adrian's name in the *Rocky II* movie.

"This is priceless." Kitty grinned.

Layla smiled but it didn't reach her eyes. "Thanks, Kitty-cat, for all your help. Don't forget to meet my sister tomorrow."

"I won't forget, I promise."

"Take care, Kitty-cat."

Before Kitty had a chance to say goodbye, Layla was gone.

Present, June 26, 2013

"So what happened next?" Dr. Morgan asked.

Kitty touched the bald spot on the back of her scalp. "As you know, Lauren and I returned all of the items that Layla stole, and Lauren and I are really tight now; I consider her my best friend. And of course I attended Layla's funeral. Obviously it was incredibly sad."

"Has Layla returned?" Dr. Morgan said.

Kitty shook her head. "Dr. Morgan, do you think I'm crazy? I mean, clearly I'm crazy, considering I see you, and I pull out my hair, and have anxiety attacks…"

Dr. Morgan gently squeezed Kitty's arm. "You are not crazy, Kitty. Layla's death has had a huge impact on you."

"But Dr. Morgan, I saw Layla. I communicated with her!"

"Some things cannot be explained. I may be a psychiatrist but that doesn't mean I don't have faith. It doesn't mean I don't believe in an after life."

Kitty fought the urge to pull strands of her hair. "Even if I'm not over the top crazy, I can't stop thinking about her. I'll be in class, taking an exam, and all of a sudden, I'm thinking of her. And I re-play that night in my head all the time. If I would have just driven her home…" Kitty whispered.

"You have to forgive yourself."

"I don't know how."

"There's nothing you can do about the past, Kitty, but there is something you can do about the future. It sounds like you've brought joy to Layla's sister and mother, and a little discomfort to Randy, which clearly, he deserves. In addition, you helped Layla tie up her loose ends so that she was able to move onto Heaven."

"I realize she's no longer here, that she's moved on, and yet it's like I'm haunted by her memory."

Kitty reaches for a strand of hair but stops midway. Instead she snaps the rubber band around her wrist.

"Have you painted any portraits of Layla?"

Kitty frowned. "No offense, Dr. Morgan, but I'm trying to stop thinking about Layla, not think about her more."

"Why don't you at least give it a try? If it doesn't work, no harm done. But you've got to move on, somehow. And if painting is your passion, it may be a wonderful avenue to move through your grief. It's time for you to tie up your loose ends."

Kitty nodded.

That evening, she perched on her window seat. Fresh paint, several brushes, and a blank canvas surrounded her. She switched on her laptop and searched for the song "If I Die Young," by the Band Perry. As the song started, Kitty dipped a brush into black paint. After she finished the portrait, she painted another, and with each one, her anxiety decreased a little more.

One day, she asked Lauren if she wanted to see the paintings.

"Woah, it's like a shrine to my sister in here." After Lauren admired each painting, she said, "This is really weird, Kitty, but it's beautiful, in a way, too. Does that make sense?"

"It makes perfect sense. Which one is your favorite?"

"This one." Lauren stood in front of the largest portrait. Layla was standing in a field of blue, her arms were outstretched, and her head was tilted toward a blue sun. Kitty had used various shades of blue to add variety and depth to the painting.

"Which one do you think your mom would like?"

Lauren pointed to a more traditional portrait.

"They're yours."

"Thank you, Kitty." Tears ran down Lauren's face but she was smiling.

A week before Kitty returned to Pittsburgh, Randy and the blonde bimbo were seated in her section at the G-Man. Kitty fought the urge to spit in his beer but she couldn't resist writing "I Know What You Did Last Summer, Randall," on the bottom of his receipt.

Scrambled Egg

When Angelica adjusts her sunglasses, Olivia notices her best friend's black eye.

"Oh, sweetie, what happened?" Olivia reaches across the sticky table for Angelica's hands but she moves them quickly; as if Olivia's touch is a flame that will burn her beyond recognition.

Angelica chews on her bottom lip. "Nothing."

"I'm worried about you."

"There's nothing to worry about, Olivia." She separates the 'O' from the 'livia.'

A spunky orange haired waitress arrives at their table. Her name tag reads "Bad Susie" with a little devil sticker next to it. "Can I take your order?"

"Plain coffee, please," Olivia says.

"Same here," Angelica says.

Susie places a hand on her hip. "You sure you don't want pancakes? Eggs and toast?"

They shake their heads.

Bad Susie tilts her head, focusing on Angelica. "You're worth so much more."

"What?" Angelica winces.

"You're wearing sunglasses indoors, long sleeves and jeans, and it's like eighty degrees outside. And your makeup is only partially covering your bruises. Obviously your boyfriend is a beater. Just know you're worth more than that." Before Angelica has a chance to respond, Susie moves to the next table.

Angelica pushes her sunglasses on top of her head, exposing a purple bruise surrounding her left eye. "Liv, did you talk to the waitress?"

"Of course not. Does it hurt?" Olivia asks softly.

"Like hell. I guess I didn't do as fabulous a makeup job as I thought." She forces a laugh.

"The waitress is right. You're worth so much more."

Angelica shrugs, brushing her friend's compliment off like the bagel crumbs that litter their table.

Bad Susie places chipped coffee mugs in front of them. "I lived with a beater, too. I walked out seven times before I finally left for good."

"What made you finally leave?" Angelica asks.

"I was afraid for our daughter. I realized that even if I didn't care enough to protect myself, I had to protect her." She fills the coffee cups. "Do you have any kids?"

"No kids," Angelica says.

"That's a blessing."

Angelica nods. "I suppose it is."

After Bad Susie leaves, Olivia asks, "What happened?" She leaves off 'this time.'

Angelica dumps three sugar packets into her cup. "He said that I was talking too much, which I probably was. He told me to shut up, I mouthed back, and then he punched me."

"You know I'm always here for you."

"I know that. You're the only one who supports me and at least tries to understand. Everyone else just tells me to leave him, like it's that easy." Angelica's phone rings.

I'm the only one who enables you, because by saying nothing, it's like I'm condoning Rob's behavior, Olivia thinks.

"Hello? I told you, I'm with Olivia. No, I won't be long. I love you too. Bye."

Rob's like a bipolar extraterrestrial. One minute he calls me a bitch and a whore and the next he's so sweet and loving. Whatever, Angelica thinks.

"What's new with you? We haven't hung out in like ages," Angelica says.

"You know same old, same old."

Angelica picks at the band aid covering her wrist, underneath is a cigarette burn from Rob. A love token of sorts.

"I've missed you in Zumba class," Olivia says.

"I've been busy, busy, busy," she lies. The truth is she has so many bruises on her body she'd have to use an entire jar of makeup to conceal them.

Bad Susie returns. "Need anything else girls? More coffee? More cream? More advice?" She chews bubble gum as if she's a cow chewing cud; a cow with a penchant for alternative music and cigarettes.

"Yes to the first offer only, please," Angelica says.

Angelica reminds Bad Susie of her former self; the self who acted so tough but in reality was so damn weak. She wants to help, but Angelica has to be willing to help herself, too.

Bad Susie fills their cups before scribbling her number on a crumpled napkin.

"In case you ever want to talk. And no, I'm not an uber-feminist or a lesbian, but I do give great advice. My name's Susie by the way."

"I'm Olivia, and that's Angelica."

"Nice to meet you both. Hope to talk to you soon, Angelica."

"God, how psycho is she?" Angelica rolls her eyes before she covers them with her sunglasses. "Let's get out of here." She drops a five dollar bill on the table before standing up.

"She just wants to help." Olivia follows her friend out of the shabby diner.

"Then why doesn't she volunteer at a women's shelter instead of badgering customers?"

"Maybe she does volunteer. Maybe you should, too. Perhaps it would open your eyes."

"Open my eyes to what? I know exactly the situation I'm in." Angelica sighs.

"I'm sorry, I know you're a grown woman and I'm not trying to control you."

"Let's change the subject because this is getting old, fast."

"Fine by me. Want to browse some thrift stores?"

Angelica's phone rings but with the surrounding city noise she doesn't hear it.

Rob's on the other line. Why the hell isn't she answering the phone? Where the hell is she? She knows she's supposed to pick up by the third ring. Dad's right, all women are worthless bitches. Just wait till she gets home, he thinks.

***

An hour later, Olivia and Angelica emerge from the basement of Kristy's Thrifties, their arms filled with bags.

Angelica checks her phone. "Crap I have like ten missed calls from Rob. My phone must have had no service in there. I've got to go."

Olivia embraces Angelica gingerly as if her body is made of soot and ash. "Do you want me to come with you?"

"No, that would make it worse; you know how cranky he gets," Angelica says.

"I can't lie, I'm afraid for you."

"I'll be fine. I love you, Liv."

"I love you, too."

***

"I thought you said you'd be back soon." Rob crushes his cigarette into an empty flower pot. It's been two weeks since he's given her flowers; they served as an apology for pulling out a chunk of her hair.

"I wasn't gone that long, Rob." Angelica places her thrift store purchases on the kitchen table.

Rob has the urge to shake her like his father shook his mother. He clenches his jaw. "Come. Here. Now."

Angelica has the urge to run but he'll only catch her, therefore she crosses the kitchen. He roughly pats the couch until she sits next to him.

His icy blue eyes narrow. "Clearly, I can't trust you. You're not allowed to go out without me any more."

"Rob, please don't."

"Don't what? Don't be a loving, protective boyfriend?"

"Is that what you call yourself?" As soon as the words cross her lips, she regrets saying them. "I'm sorry, I didn't mean it!"

Rob raises his fist and punches her in the jaw.

***

The next morning, Angelica pretends to sleep as Rob crushes his lips to her forehead.

"I'm sorry, pretty baby. Just be a good girl from now on." He lightly strokes her jaw before leaving for work. She waits until the front door closes before she phones her boss.

"Hi, Annie." She coughs. "I think I have the flu, so I won't be in today. I know, only I would get the flu in July. Yes, I'll definitely be in tomorrow, thanks."

She takes the hottest shower possible, even though it's eighty-six degrees in the apartment. She pulls on a white long sleeved tee shirt, jeans and flip flops. Fortunately her feet aren't bruised. Then she opens her laptop and googles 'Women's Shelters.' The closest shelter is eight blocks away. It's the only shelter in the city.

***

Angelica hesitates before she opens the door to the shelter. She's surprised to find the waiting room empty; for some reason she imagined the room filled with crying, battered women. Metal folding chairs align the perimeter of the room. The walls are painted mauve with teal trim; very nineteen-nineties. She takes a step back, reconsidering what exactly is she doing there?

"How can I help you, sugar?" A curly haired woman rises from behind the front desk.

"Um, I need community service hours for school, so I thought maybe I could volunteer here?" Angelica is amazed at how quickly she came up with a lie.

"It looks like you could use some help. What's that mark on your wrist?" Shelby asks softly.

"Oh, this?" Angelica rubs her wrist. "It's a cigarette burn; I'm really clumsy when I smoke. I usually wear a band aid."

Shelby's eyes narrow. "How long has he been beating you?"

"Is it that apparent?" She pushes her glasses on top of her head. "I thought I was good at disguising it but I guess not."

"We all think we're good at hiding our pain, sugar, but not many of us can pull it off. I'm Shelby and you must be Angelica."

Angelica frowns. "How did you know my name?"

"Bad Susie was hoping that you'd either call her or stop by here. She already told me a little bit about you."

Angelica backs away from the desk. "You have me mistaken for someone else."

"I don't think so, sugar. I shouldn't have mentioned that Bad Susie was talking about you but she means well. In fact, she's helped so many women at this shelter. She's been volunteering here for seven years."

"Olivia was right."

"Who's Olivia?" Shelby asks, scrunching her nose.

"Just a friend."

"Oh. Would you like some breakfast? Everyone's eating now."

A cup of coffee would help, she thinks. "Umm, okay."

Angelica follows Shelby into a congested but sunny room filled with women and children.

"Grab a tray." Shelby motions to the stack of orange plastic trays.

"What kind of egg are you feeling like today? Scrambled, or sunny side up?" A petite woman asks. Even with the hair net and silly cap, she's pretty.

"Umm, definitely scrambled, please," Angelica says.

"Sunny side up for me, please." Shelby grins.

They fill the rest of their trays with sausage links, toast, orange juice, and coffee. At the end of the line, Shelby says, "I have to return to my post. Why don't you have a seat and introduce yourself to some of these fabulous women."

Angelica feels like the new kid at school as she slinks to the end of a crowded table. What is she doing here? She plans on eating as quickly as possible before escaping out the nearest door.

"Hi, I'm Jessica." A dark skinned woman sits next to her.

"I'm Angelica."

"What a pretty name. Are you new here?"

She takes a long sip of coffee before answering. "Actually, I'd like to volunteer."

"That's the excuse a lot of us have used."

"It's not an excuse; I really want to volunteer." Maybe if she says it enough, she'll start to believe it herself.

"I didn't mean to offend you. It's just that you've got to help yourself before you can help anyone else. Do you know Bad Susie?"

"Just met her yesterday. Why does she go by 'Bad Susie'?"

"Because she's a bad ass against domestic violence."

Angelica folds her arms tightly across her chest. "I hate the term 'domestic violence,' as if we're cows or something."

"Moo." Jessica grins and takes a sip of orange juice. "I'd rather be a cow than a steak; think about it. Want to know why I'm here?"

"Okay."

"My ex, the a-hole, threw me down the stairs when I was seven months pregnant. He left me there to die. My baby died instead."

"I am so sorry."

"You will be if you stay in your relationship." She checks her watch. "Time for group therapy. Should I save you a seat?"

Angelica nods even though she has no intention of joining a group of any kind. She sits in the cafeteria until everyone is gone. Then she dumps her tray and exits through the back door. Assaulted by sunlight, she plops on a bench before she bursts into tears. She thinks about all of the times that Rob had stabbed her with a fork, bitten her so hard that he's drawn blood, and branded her with cigarettes. He's even held a knife to her throat. Perhaps she is a cow on the way to a slaughter house.

"Angelica, are you okay?" Bad Susie sits beside her.

She shakes her head. "I don't want to be a dead piece of meat. I need help."

"Then you came to the right place. Think of it this way; a person in an abusive relationship is similar to a drying starfish, the abuser is like the shore, and the sea is representative of freedom from the abuse. Often the only way for the starfish to return to the sea is by asking for help."

"That's a very cool analogy."

"It is, isn't it?" Bad Susie says. She tries not to think of the thousands of star fish left to dry along the shore.

"I'm so proud of you, Angelica." Olivia sits beside her and gently places her arm around her friend's shoulders. She notices small bruises on her neck. Angelica is beginning to look like an egg shell after it's been dipped in purple and blue food coloring.

"How did you know I was here?" Angelica says.

"Shelby called Bad Susie, and then Bad Susie called me. I slipped her my number at the diner," Olivia says.

"I'm glad you're here." Angelica sighs. "I don't want to stay at this shelter but I know that I need to leave Rob."

"Stay with me," Olivia says.

"Does Rob know where you live?" Bad Susie asks. Olivia nods. "Then that's not the best idea. Why don't you stay with me? Rob doesn't know where I live."

"But I don't even know you. Why would you let me stay at your home?" Angelica asks.

"I needed help once, too. Now I'm paying it forward." Bad Susie says.

"Thanks for the offer, but I'd rather stay with Olivia," Angelica says.

"If you do that, Rob will know where to find you. He'll bang on the door and plead for you to come back," Bad Susie says. "Believe me; I've seen this happen over and over again."

"Just until Rob gives up and then you can move in with me," Olivia says.

"I'm afraid he'll never give up… but okay," Angelica says.

"Let's swing by your apartment to collect your things," Olivia says.

"Fortunately, most of it's his anyway," Angelica says.

As they walk the eight blocks to Angelica's apartment, they pass four bars.

There's only one women's shelter in the entire city yet there are dozens of bars. In fact, The Happy Hour bar is right next to the apartment building.

Angelica's hands shake so much she has trouble opening her front door.

"Here, let me." Olivia takes her friend's keys and unlocks the door. "Sweetie, it's going to be okay."

"Where's your suitcase?" Bad Susie asks.

"In the hall closet. Grab his, too. I might as well get something out of this relationship," Angelica says bitterly. In turn, Olivia hugs her.

Bad Susie carries the suitcases into the living room. "Fortunately, these are huge."

Bad Susie helps Angelica fill Rob's suitcase with books while Olivia gathers Angelica's toiletries and clothes.

"At least we don't have pets." Tears run down Angelica's face.

"Or worse, children," Bad Susie says.

"That's a good point."

Olivia carries Angelica's suitcase into the living room. "You about ready?"

Angelica nods. "Should I leave a note?"

"That's up to you," Bad Susie says.

Angelica grabs a sticky note and pen. She bites her lip for a minute before she writes. She sticks the note to the refrigerator.

Bad Susie asks, "Do you have his cell number memorized?"

"No, but it's in my phone." Angelica pulls her phone from her back pocket.

"You need to delete it," Bad Susie says.

"Delete it? But that's so permanent," Angelica says.

Bad Susie shoots her a look. "And this isn't?"

"Another good point. Okay." Angelica scrolls through her contacts and stops on Rob's. Memories of the good times flash through her mind. But then she glances at her wrist and sees the cigarette burn. She deserves better than this. She hits DELETE.

"Let's go," she says.

***

A little after five o'clock, Rob walks through the door. "Angel baby, I'm home. What's for dinner?" He walks through the apartment yelling her name. In the bathroom, he notices that all of her toiletries are missing. Next, he thrusts open the hall closet to find both suitcases gone.

"I can't believe that ungrateful bitch left me, after all I've done for her!" Rob yells. He paces through the apartment until he settles in the kitchen. He decides a beer is all he really needs.

Then he notices a note stuck on the refrigerator that reads: "You're a Deviled Egg and I'm Scrambled but soon I'll be Sunny Side Up."

The Collector

"Pthu, pthu, pthu! Mom, I swallowed a spider! Pthu!" I scrape a crumpled tissue across my tongue until I realize it's been used.

Mom lifts her head from her pillow as if it weighs as much as Licorice, our black Labrador retriever, and glances at me. "What time is it?"

"It's eight-fifteen."

"Alright, time to get up." Mom makes it two steps before she bangs her foot on a toaster oven. "Ouch!" She weaves through alternate dirty and clean mounds of clothes before perching on my twin bed. "How did you manage to swallow a spider?"

"It must have crawled into my water glass, I think it was a daddy longlegs. I swallowed the body and the legs were on my tongue, pthu!"

"Did you know that there are daddy longlegs, which belong to the order Opiliones because they are not actual spiders and daddy longleg spiders which are in the Pholcidae family?"

"Whatever, I need to brush my teeth!" I untangle myself from the covers and cautiously creep through towers of science fiction and fantasy books which nearly block the entrance to our bathroom.

***

"Mmm, smells like cinnamon. John, did you make French toast?"
I ask my grandmother's second husband. My mother says that
John married Grandma because she's a "nurse with a purse." He
retired early and just hangs out at the house all day while Mom
and Grandma work twelve hour shifts at the hospital. At least he
can cook. I slide onto a kitchen chair and take a swig of orange
juice. "Even though I just brushed my teeth, this still tastes better
than the daddy longlegs."

"What are you talking about?" Grandma purses her coral
colored lips which mom refers to as 'fish lips' behind her back.

"I swallowed one this morning, it was in my water glass.
Blech!"

Grandma shoots Mom a look. "I don't even want to think
about how many other insects are crawling around upstairs."

Mom rolls her eyes and reaches for the syrup.

John plops French toast onto each of our plates before
pouring everyone but Licorice and I a cup of coffee.

"When can I drink coffee?"

"When you're twelve," John replies.

"Well then in four months you'll be pouring me coffee."

"Four months? Diana, Samantha really ought to have her own
bedroom. Wouldn't you like that, Samantha?" Grandma asks.

I glance at Mom, who's shoveling French toast into her
mouth, before replying. "That might be cool."

"Diana, you're off today, right? Why don't you start cleaning
out one of the spare bedrooms?" asks Grandma.

"Would that make everyone at this table happy?" Mom asks
and we all nod our heads.

***

After breakfast, John takes Licorice for her Sunday walk along
the nearby nature trail. Like a baby duck, I follow Mom and
Grandma to the third floor which John and Grandma avoid like
the morgue. Their bedroom is on the second floor therefore Mom
and I have the entire pig pen to muck up.

"An arsonist's dream." Grandma mutters as we pass stacks of
newspapers and magazines littering each step. "Maybe we should
just light a match," she adds. At the landing, Grandma motions to

one of the closed doors. "Why don't you choose this one, Samantha? There's an extra window."

"Okay." I push my body against the door and it opens a few inches before it sticks.

"Here's the game plan. We'll fill this box with things that Diana wants to keep, this box with donations for charity and this one with trash," Grandma places sizeable boxes against the wall. "Boxes, unlike newspapers from the seventies, are always handy."

"Mom, give it a rest," my mother says.

The first item I grab through the narrow space is one of Licorice's tattered dog toys, which I toss in the 'trash' box.

"Licorice may still want that toy, Sammie." Mom says.

"But the squeaker's gone. She never plays with toys once the squeakers are ripped out…" A look of panic crosses her face like a bolt of lightening streaking across the sky.

I pull the dog toy from the 'trash' and place it in the 'keep' box.

Grandma drops a mitten into the 'trash' box.

"Mom, I'm sure the mitten's twin is somewhere in the room. We need to keep that."

Grandma stares at Mom while chewing on the inside of her right cheek.

"Umm, Grandma, do you have another box that we can label 'maybe?' I ask.

"That's a great idea, Sammie." Mom smiles.

"I'll bring another box but I don't think I can be of any further help here," Grandma says.

As Grandma walks downstairs, mom purses her lips, sticks out her breasts and says, "I can see that my help is not appreciated," in a perfect Grandma Ruth impersonation.

I crack up laughing.

***

After two hours, the 'keep' and 'maybe' boxes are spilling over with Mom's ancient tap shoes, outdated nursing text books, my old coloring books and crayon stubs, and other useless things.

The 'donation' box contains a few tee shirts and the 'trash' is empty.

"We need a break. Want to go for ice cream?" Mom's face is smudged with newspaper ink, her dyed auburn hair is pulled back in a messy bun, and she's wearing yellow scrubs decorated with sleeping sheep.

"Of course."

***

I throw several Styrofoam cups and empty fast food bags in the backseat before climbing into Mom's yellow Ford Fiesta that she's had since before I was born. She winds her window down a crack, turns the radio on full blast and sings off-key along with some really old song about saving time in a bottle. At the stop sign she rubs her eyes and sniffs.

"What's wrong?"

"Just allergies, honey." She pats me on the head.

I slouch in the passenger seat as Mom drives along Main Street. When we pass Susie's house, she asks, "How come you don't hang out with Susie any more? She seems like such a nice girl. You know your friends are always welcome. I don't know why you never invite them over."

Susie isn't a nice girl but I don't want to get into it with Mom. In first grade, I was invited to Susie's birthday party. "Where's all of your mom's collectibles?" I had asked, as I walked through her house, which was so white and barren it reminded me of a hospital. She shrugged before shrieking about a moon bounce in the backyard.

A few weeks later, I invited Susie to my house to play.

"Why do you have trash in your house?" She asked.

"It's not trash, they're Mom's collectibles."

"But it looks like trash." She wrinkled her nose.

At recess the next day, Susie announced, "Sammie's mom collects trash!"

For the rest of first grade, Susie's clique called me 'Garbage Girl.'

***

"Wow, no one's at 'The Cow,' Mom says when we pull into the deserted parking lot.

"That's because it's freezing out. And it's October."

"I thought you wanted ice cream?"

"I do Mom, sorry."

Larry, who owns 'The Cow,' smiles like a deranged clown as we approach. "Customers, yes!" He says with a fist pump. Mom feels sorry for him because he's a widower but I think he's a creeper.

"I really need to start selling coffee and chili! What can I get for you two pretty ladies?"

"Can I please have a medium mint chocolate chip cone?" I ask.

"Make that two, please," Mom says.

I rub my arms and hop from one foot to another. "I'd sit in the car but I'm afraid to leave you alone with the ice cream man."

Mom shakes her head.

Larry pops his head out the window with massive cones. "I took the liberty of making you supersized sugar cones."

"But we ordered mediums," Mom says.

"No charge for the free upgrade. Ha, ha, ha. For you two pretty ladies, it's on the house."

"Are you sure?" Mom asks.

"Just promise you'll visit again soon." He winks and his left eyebrow wiggles like a caterpillar.

"Thank you," we say. Then we quickly walk to the car.

"You're right, he's a creeper." Mom whispers before she takes a large bite of ice cream.

"Kids can be right too, you know."

"You're not a kid anymore, Sammie. You're growing into a phenomenal young woman. Promise me you won't date a creeper." A single tear races down her freckled cheek.

"Mom, you're really emotional today. Are you on your period?"

"Can't I just love my Sammie?" She hugs me to her side before we get back into the car.

***

I've never met my father. Mom has never dated anyone since Jerry, who fled hick town soon after she told him she was pregnant with me. Grandma says that kids need a father but Mom argues that I'm better off without a father than with a dead beat like Jerry. My mom says she agrees with Grandma but sometimes I catch her gazing at their prom picture. I just know the song about saving time in a bottle was their song since she listens to it constantly. I guess it's only Mom's song now.

***

After our ice cream run, progress is minimal: the 'keep' and 'maybe' boxes expand but the 'trash' and 'donate' boxes remains as empty as my piggy bank.

"Aww, look at this." Mom waves a tattered Valentine's Day heart in my face. "You made this in kindergarten."

"Ugh, throw it out. Look at all the misspelled words."

"That's what makes it special." She holds the construction card heart to her chest.

"Are you an alien? Where's my real mom? Because my mom is not this sappy."

"Just wait until you have children, Sammie."

"Nah, I'll just have dogs."

"You say that now. How about we stop for today? Want to make popcorn with extra butter and watch a movie? We haven't watched *Lord of the Rings* in a while."

"Yay, Mom's back."

***

I empathize more and more with Grandma each time Mom and I work on the bedroom project. Mom refuses to throw away things like plastic containers from Chinese food restaurants.

"You never know when one comes in handy," she says.

One afternoon, while Mom's busy counting empty fruit cups, I toss numerous books covered in mildew in the 'trash' box. I attempt to sneak outside to the garbage bin and throw them away.

"Sammie, what are you doing with the 'trash' box?" Her hands are on her hips and she's biting her lip. "I thought we had a deal that you'd check with me first?"

"Mom, these books have mildew on them."

Regardless, she roots trough the garbage bin.

"These books are perfectly salvageable." She grips a handful of yellowed books speckled with mildew.

"I'm never going to have a room of my own because you'll never throw anything away."

My mother takes a deep breath and says, "You're right and I'm sorry," and drops the books into the garbage bin.

That evening, Mom returns this trash to the bookcase in my new room. And I realize as I look around the room, we've been organizing useless junk this entire time. Susie was right, Mom doesn't own collectibles, she owns a landfill.

***

I don't realize how sick Mom really is until one week before she dies. She keeps repeating, "Nasty case of pneumonia, as soon as spring arrives, we'll finish our project…"

***

During Mom's last week all she wants is mint chocolate chip ice cream therefore John and I make frequent trips to 'The Cow.' The creeper doesn't charge us and he always asks about Mom's health. I bet he really misses his wife.

***

Mom rests her eyes a lot, so I read to her, mostly books by J. R. Tolken. She jokes that Grandma no longer acts like a sarcastic broad. Licorice refuses to leave Mom's side unless it's to pee on her favorite oak tree. John finds odd jobs in town and Grandma takes a leave of absence from the hospital.

***

I refuse to wear black to Mom's funeral because she hated that color. Instead I wear a yellow sun dress even though it's January. Grandma doesn't protest when I choose a similar dress for Mom. Yellow was her favorite color after all.

***

I return to school a week after the funeral. I feel numb and guilty because I haven't shed a single tear. How can secretaries at my school who barely knew my mom cry, when I can't? But maybe they're not crying for Mom, maybe their tears are for me.

I overhear Tommy, the class bully, say, "Who wants to bet that Sammie starts collecting trash, too?"

"Shut up, Tommy." Susie, my former friend and the most popular girl in our class, says.

He listens.

***

On February first, I wake to find Grandma stroking my hair. "Your birthday is in less than two weeks, Samantha. How about we clean that bedroom for you?"

"But I want to stay in this bedroom."

"That's fine, honey. Can you please help me clean this room?"

"Okay but where do we start?"

"That's the million dollar question. Let's start with these vinyls." She holds up *Janis Joplin's Greatest Hits*.

"We can't get rid of Mom's records."

Janis returns to the stack.

"How about these paperbacks?"

"But Mom loved those books. Can't we just get rid of garbage instead of Mom's collectibles?" For the first time since she died, tears pour down my face. "I don't want to forget her."

"Samantha, your mother's spirit isn't in these materials, she's in your heart." She places her hand on my chest. "Your mom suffered from a mental illness, honey. Deep down she knew what she was doing was bizarre but she couldn't help herself. Why not give a lot of her collectibles to charity so that others may enjoy what she loved so much?"

"Are you going to put me in the charity box?" I sniff.

"No way, you're a keeper."

***

It takes the entire ten days to paint the walls a lemon yellow color, decontaminate, and decorate the bedroom. My comforter and curtains are light yellow with white polka dots, I have a new full size bed and a white desk and chair. I'm twelve-years-old and I finally have a room of my own. I'm twelve-years-old and my mother is dead and I've never met my father.

Grandma, John, Licorice and I celebrate my birthday at home. John makes my favorite dinner: spaghetti and meat balls and a vanilla cake with sugary frosting. They do their best to cheer me up but Mom's space at the table is empty and always will be.

After dinner, I fall face down on my bed and sob, bite, and holler into my pillow until my voice disappears. When I finally sit up and reach for my water glass, I notice a daddy longlegs spider balancing on the edge.

EVEN IN DEATH

What's Really There

No one ever wants to see what's really there.

We live in the country, three hundred miles from the closest beach, and yet their sadness crashes precisely like waves against the shore. My husband David and I felt their presence early on, within a few weeks of buying their home. At first it was tolerable, although a bit cramped; two people and three ghosts sharing 1,000 square feet. But we got used to them; footsteps in the attic, windows creaking open in the dead of night, occasional sighs and sniffles; but that was before they started touching us.

Mrs. Horner touched me three times when she was alive.

On a Saturday in September, 2005, our realtor phoned. Sam was adamant that he had found the perfect house for us, even though it wasn't a Colonial, didn't have a garage, or a master bath. As I was about to say "no thanks," Sam gently reminded me that based on our minimal budget, David and I had to compromise.

Later that day, Sam, David, and I had just stepped out of Sam's SUV when we heard a raspy female voice say, "Realtor, bring the couple down to say hello." Beneath an oak tree an elderly couple swayed on a wooden swing.

"The owners are here? That's awkward," David said.

Sam shrugged. "They insisted."

We descended the stone steps into a storybook backyard; red and blue birds splashed in bird baths, plump Autumn Gold apples hung from trees, and chrysanthemums in nearly every color of the rainbow bloomed.

"This yard is gorgeous," I said.

"It takes a lot of hard work and a lot of time to care for two acres. You'll be giving up plenty of Saturdays to maintain my yard," the elderly gentleman said. With his wrinkled face and tan skin, it was clear that he did in fact spend a lot of time outdoors.

David and I exchanged a 'what have we gotten into' look.

"Don't mind him; he's wearing his grumpy pants today. I'm Betty Horner and this is my husband Jeff." We introduced ourselves and shook hands. Compared to her husband's, Betty's skin was smooth and milky white.

"Please have a seat, and help yourselves to some apple cider. We use our own apples." Betty motioned to a pitcher of amber colored liquid and glasses.

"Thank you. I've been craving something sweet," I said.

While Betty asked David and me a plethora of questions, Jeff inhaled cigarettes as fast as I devour Hershey Kisses.

As if reading my mind, Betty said, "We've never smoked indoors."

Relieved, I nodded. I grew up in a home with yellowed walls and ceilings and no matter how many coats of white paint my parents applied, yellow spots from smokers past would creep back.

"So where are you moving to?" Sam asked.

"Ocala, Florida, near our son, Mark. Sunshine, oranges, horses, and family, what more could we wish for?" Betty smiled, but it didn't meet her eyes.

"I don't share my wife's excitement. I'm content right where I am." Jeff spread his arms wide.

Sam glanced at his watch. "Are you ready to take a look at the house?"

David and I rose quickly whereas Betty and Jeff stood slowly.

"It was nice meeting you, David," Betty said. They shook hands before she clasped mine. "And Sara, I do hope you buy our home. It's the perfect place for children; in fact, we raised three."

David and I laughed. "Not for a few more years," I said.

"Not years, months." Betty placed her hands on my stomach. "Sara, you're expecting."

I shook my head. "No, I've just gained some weight. Since my knee injury I haven't been able to exercise much."

"Don't mind her, she's wearing her chatter lips today," Jeff said.

Betty pinched Jeff lightly on his arm and fake pouted.

"It was nice meeting you both, you're a fine couple." He shook our hands. "You can enter through the garage, its open."

As we headed towards their house, Betty lowered her voice. "Jeff, doesn't she remind you of Janice?"

"Well, with that red hair she doesn't look like her, but she's pleasant like your sister was," Jeff said.

I whispered, "Sam, I thought you said there wasn't a garage."

"Well there is, but it's not used as one." He pointed. A garage was attached to the rear of the house, however, the steep hill made it impossible to utilize.

"What a strange design. Who built it?" David asked.

"Mr. Horner built this home in 1955, but please don't write it off yet." Sam opened the garage door which emitted a bouquet of smells: fresh cut grass, gasoline, and tires. It reminded me of lazy Saturdays with my father. I took a few deep breaths before I followed David and Sam into the basement.

"I forgot to mention, the riding lawn mower and the rest of the tools in the garage convey. So does the washer, dryer, and two freezers." Sam pointed to the appliances. "Over here, there's a three piece washroom."

"Who would want to shower in here?" I scrunched my nose at the cement floor, faded shower curtain, and pastel yellow bathroom fixtures.

David replied, "We can always renovate the bathroom and finish the basement. In fact, I'm envisioning a man cave." He wandered around the dim space. "There's room down here for a bar, pool table, juke box; the possibilities are endless."

"I'm sure the cost is endless, too." I couldn't help but smile at his enthusiasm.

"Let's head upstairs. I think you're really going to like it," Sam said.

At the top of the stairs, Sam flung open the door which led to the kitchen. "Isn't this kitchen fabulous?"

"Actually, it is," I said, surprised. "What kind of wood is this?"

"It's called knotty pine and the walls are flagstone," Sam said.

"It's like we stepped back in time. Has anything been replaced?" David asked.

"No, it's all original. Well maintained though," Sam said.

The upper cabinet doors were removed which allowed the bright plates and knick knacks to pop. The black and white checkerboard flooring and white appliances added color to the predominantly wooden room.

"Check this out." Sam veered to the left. David and I followed him into a cozy room with large bay windows and light pink walls. It reminded me of a homemade Valentine's Day card from my niece. I loved it.

"This is where Sara will spend all her time," David said.

"This is a newer addition that Betty wanted. They call it the 'pink room,'" Sam said.

"This is perfect for my sewing and crafts." I clasped my hands together.

David drew up the blinds. "What a view," he said. We gazed into the backyard for several moments until Sam broke the spell.

"Let's continue," he said.

There was a charming living room, three decent size bedrooms and a full bathroom but it was the backyard, kitchen and pink room that won me over.

"So, what do you think?" Sam looked expectantly at David and me.

In unison we said, "We'll take it!"

At the end of November, we moved in. The Horners left some of their furniture behind, including an old fashioned curio cabinet. One day while I was dusting it, David asked if there were any items left in the drawers.

"Not yet, but I have one more drawer to check." I pulled open the highest drawer on the right and reached in. At the back of the drawer, my fingers brushed something smooth, wooden, and in the shape of a T. I lifted the object out. "David, check this out." I placed the cross in his palm.

He rubbed the cross. "This is a comfort cross, made of olive wood. Some people caress them during prayers but I'll hang it in our bedroom for good luck."

We spent the next few weeks cleaning, painting, and scouring antique shops in order to make our house a home. We were so busy that I didn't realize I was out of birth control pills until I swallowed the last one. In fact, the label read 'O refills'. When I phoned my doctor's office for a refill, I was asked to make an appointment for the yearly pap smear.

"We had a cancellation for three o'clock this afternoon, if that's convenient for you," the receptionist said.

The only thing worse than a pap smear is a trip to the dentist when you have a mouthful of cavities; but I didn't have much of a choice. "That works well, thank you."

That afternoon I left the doctor's office feeling contradictory emotions including joy, sadness, and shock. It was if each of these emotions had been poured into a blender, mixed, and then given to me to choke down. Betty was right, I was three months pregnant. When I asked the doctor how it was possible, considering I just ran out of birth control pills; she said there are many reasons why this occurs and that several of her patients have become pregnant while taking the pill.

I wanted to be a mother, just not a twenty-six-year-old mother. My whole life I've been a planner and having a baby was supposed to wait until I was at least thirty. But fate had other plans and one thing I was certain of; I would love this baby like nothing I've ever loved before. I prayed that David would feel the same way.

On the way home, to cushion the blow, I stopped by the local ice cream shop where I chose a round ice cream cake. I asked them to write "Congratulations, Daddy!" in blue and pink frosting. Next, I ordered an antipasto salad and two chicken parmesan dinners from our favorite Italian restaurant.

As soon as David walked through the front door, he said, "Smells heavenly, must be takeout."

I stuck out my tongue. "Very funny."

"Red or white wine with dinner? I think a large glass of wine will alleviate my headache. It's been a rough day." He removed his suit jacket and tossed it on the couch before collapsing into a kitchen chair.

I opened a bottle of Merlot and poured him a glass before joining him at the table. He didn't notice that my hands were shaking or that I didn't pour one for myself.

"Do you want to talk about it?"

"No, it's just work crap. But I do have some bad news. The Horner's' son called earlier to tell me that Betty and Jeff were in a fatal car accident this morning. Evidently Jeff had a stroke while driving. He died instantly and Betty soon after." He ran his hands through his dark hair.

"That's horrible."

David squeezed my hands. "Mark said they had a very happy life together. And that's all any of us can wish for, right?"

"Absolutely, but it's still so sad."

"I hate to sound insensitive but I'm starving." He took a large bite of antipasto salad. "This needs some more dressing." David walked to the fridge and opened the door.

"There's a bottle on the right side," I said.

"Is this an ice cream cake? What's the occasion?"

My heart flipped in my chest like a fish. "I was going to save the surprise until after dinner, but go ahead and read the cake."

He pulled the cake out of the fridge and stared at it for a long moment. "Wow. How far along are you?"

"Three months." I stood and touched my belly.

He placed the cake on the counter before he embraced me. "What great news."

I stepped back. "Really? You're not mad or scared or something?"

"No, I'm happy, shocked but happy. Let's start a list of everything our baby needs. And we'll have to decide which bedroom would make the best nursery..."

I laughed. "Can we have dinner first? I'm eating for two, you know."

"Good idea." He slid back in his chair.

"Honey, you forgot the dressing."

"Yeah, the cake distracted me a bit." He grinned.

***

In the following months, we spent every moment of our free time pouring over baby books and preparing the nursery. So far my pregnancy had been relatively easy, except for the insomnia. Most nights I woke at three am. One night I woke David when I thought I heard the sound of furniture moving across the attic.

"It's an old house, it's just settling," he said.

But I knew it wasn't the house making noise because eventually I noticed a pattern. Every three nights I would wake to the sound of furniture being dragged across the attic. I was so freaked out that I made David search the attic.

"What am I looking for?"

"I don't know, something supernatural, I guess."

Half an hour later, he climbed down the flimsy wooden steps, covered in dirt and dust. "I found a boat load of things for the nursery: antique furniture, clothes, and toys. Some of it just requires some TLC. Should I bring some of the boxes down?"

"No, leave it where it is, please. I don't want anything that belongs to a ghost!"

"Ghosts aren't real, sweetheart."

But I knew that ghosts were in fact real. Every three days, I'd feel a female spirit watching me, especially when I looked into a mirror. And every three days, I woke to sounds in the attic. But I wasn't terrified until three days later, when the comfort cross was moved. David was the first to notice it.

"Sara, why did you turn the cross sideways? Were you cleaning?"

"What are you talking about? I haven't touched the cross since I found it." But there it was, pointing sideways.

David straightened it. "It's not a good omen to turn a cross sideways."

When he noticed my glare, he said, "I'm not saying it was you. It could have been me."

Three days later, David discovered the cross under the bed. Three days after that, I found it in the closet.

"I'm really scared," I said.

"I'll ask my mother to have it blessed," he said.

That Sunday David's mother returned the cross. "No need to worry any longer. Father Clemens blessed it."

I wish I could say that the blessing worked.

"What should we do?" I asked.

"Let's put it back where we found it." He lifted it from the wall and returned it to the curio cabinet. "Maybe it's not the cross, maybe it's the house. I'll ask my mom to bring holy water from the church."

That evening, she rang the bell which she's never done before; usually she lets herself in.

"Here you go, dear." She handed David a spray bottle.

"Thanks, Mom. Would you like to come in?"

She peered over David's shoulder, as if looking for our resident ghosts. "No, I best get home. Bye." She pecked David on the cheek and waved at me before she scurried down the steps. David immediately sprayed the holy water throughout our house.

Three days later, I found the cross in our baby's crib.

"That's it, we're moving!" I said.

"Let's try a psychic first," he said quietly.

"So now you believe in ghosts?"

"Looks that way."

"How do you know a legitimate psychic?"

"I've done some research."

The earliest the psychic could come was in three weeks, on April 6th. In the meantime, the spirits started touching us. Every three nights, I'd feel a hand stroke my hair and David felt a soft kiss on his forehead. Neither of us could sleep and bags formed under our eyes.

In addition, my panic attacks returned with a vengeance; complete with racing thoughts, rapid heart beats, and difficulty breathing. As a teen, I was prescribed Prozac for general anxiety and depression but had gradually weaned myself off of it. I felt like creating a tee shirt that read: 'Antidepressant Free For Eight Years. Leave Me Alone So I can Stay That Way.'

However, after a particularly awful evening in which I begged David to drive me to the hospital because I was convinced I was having a heart attack; I reconsidered taking some kind of medication. The empathetic ER doctor agreed and prescribed a daily dose of 40mg of Prozac. He assured me that Prozac was safer for the baby than my nightly panic attacks.

But the worst part was when a rancid odor filled my nose. It was like opening the lid of a Tupperware container, left way too long in the refrigerator. David didn't smell a thing. Three days later, I received a call from my father, telling me that my aunt Margaret had died. It was if I smelled death approaching my aunt like a putrid black cloak.

***

"Billy's here," David said, peering out the living room window.

"Let me see...he looks like a baby." His face was round and spotted with acne.

"He's eighteen and highly reputable, I swear."

I watched as Billy lifted equipment from the trunk of his Toyota Scion. A petite brunette climbed out of the passenger seat.

"Looks like he brought a girlfriend, too," David said.

"If she wore less eyeliner, she'd really be cute. By the way, how much is he charging?"

"Fifty bucks."

"That's it?"

"He's just starting out, give him a break."

"Who recommended him?"

"My mother," David said. That shut me up. I followed him to the door.

"Hi, I'm Billy and this is my friend Marissa." He extended his free hand and we shook. Marissa simply nodded.

"I'm David and this is my wife, Sara. Please come in."

Billy and Marissa sat on the couch closest to the window and David and I settled on the loveseat against the wall. I was about to ask if they wanted something to drink when I noticed their slime green Gatorade bottles.

"I'll explain everything to you before I do it. In case you're wondering, Marissa isn't psychic. However, I don't like entering homes alone, it doesn't seem safe," Billy said.

"But if you're psychic, wouldn't you know if a home was safe or not, before hand?" I asked. From the corner of my eye, I noticed David frowning.

"With all due respect, ma'am, I'm a medium, not a fortune teller."

"I'm sorry; I suppose I don't understand the difference."

"A medium is able to communicate between the dead and the living. A fortune teller predicts information about a person's life. Today I'll be conducting a psychic reading on your house."

I nodded.

"First, I'd like to show you the tools I use." He opened a large tote bag and pulled out a small voice recorder. "I'll be recording our session because sometimes sounds are caught on recordings that we don't hear during the recording. It's called EVP- Electronic Voice Phenomenon." Next he held up a small meter. "I'll also be using an EMF meter which measures electronic magnetic energy, including spirit energy." Marissa pulled out a notebook, thermometer and camera. "I'll also take notes, measure the temperature, and take pictures. Do you have any questions so far?"

David and I shook our heads.

Billy dropped his head and closed his eyes. Marissa returned the tools to the tote bag.

"What's he doing?" I asked Marissa.

"He's asking the spirits for permission to be here."

When Billy opened his eyes, he was smiling. He stood and clasped his hands. "First we'll open all of the doors and curtains."

When he noticed my wrinkled expression, he explained. "Spirits like to hide in closets and behind curtains. Even shower curtains."

Marissa and I remained in the living room while David and Billy played hide and seek with the spirits. When they returned, Billy turned on the voice recorder and the meter. Marissa opened the notebook and handed it to him.

"Let's begin here in the living room. Why don't you tell me a bit about what's been going on."

For the next half hour David and I described the strange occurrences.

Billy held up three fingers. "The number three symbolizes the past, present, and future. It's also the number of spirits that are haunting this house: one man and two women."

A chill ran down my spine.

"It's very common for spirits to move objects but from my experience, crosses only move in one out of ten houses."

Billy stood and turned toward the bay window. "He stands here at night. In fact, he starts in the master bedroom, walks to the window, looks out, and then exits through the basement. He does this every three nights."

"Who is he?" I whispered.

"Jeff Horner. You remind him of his daughter and he strokes your hair at night."

"Why is he here?" I asked.

"Because this is his Heaven. Do you want to ask him to leave?"

"I don't want to do that, if it's his Heaven, but I would like him to stop touching my hair and making so much noise."

"He's not the one making noise nor is his wife, Betty. She's ready to move on to the afterlife, but she stays to watch over Jeff. She doesn't bother you at all."

"Then who is the one moving the cross and making all the racket?" I asked.

Just then, David's musical birthday card played the Beatle's "Birthday" song.

David jumped from the love seat and flailed his arms and legs. "I'm seriously freaked out. I don't know how much more I can take."

"It's okay, we're here to help," Marissa said quietly.

I gently tugged David's arm until he sat back down.

Billy lifted the card from the end table. "It's Janice Campbell. She's the spirit whose been making all of the noise. She's Betty's younger sister."

"Why is she here? Is this her Heaven, too?" I asked.

"No, but she feels compelled to stay here because this is where her baby died."

"What did her baby die from? And shouldn't her baby be in Heaven?" I asked, placing a hand on my belly.

"Janice says her baby was a stillborn and yes, he's in Heaven."

"Then wouldn't she want to be with him?" I asked.

Billy sighed. "It's complicated."

"How do we get her to leave? Is she evil?" David asked.

Billy shook his head. "There's nothing evil in this house, only sadness. If I felt any evil, I'd make the sign of the cross under each doorway. You'll have to talk to her and convince her to leave. That's the only way to get rid of a spirit." He closed his eyes for a moment before asking if he could see the attic.

"Sure, it's over here." David pulled the attic steps into the hallway.

Marissa and David followed Billy up the attic steps, whereas I stood at the bottom.

"Come up here, sweetie," David said.

"But the steps are rickety."

"I want you to see this, it's important. Be careful."

I climbed slowly up the wooden stairs. When I reached the top, I gasped. An entire nursery was set up in the attic. The rocking chair was empty, yet it rocked back and forth.

"Don't touch anything, it may stir more spirits if you do," Billy said.

Marissa held up the thermometer. "It's ten degrees colder up here." Then she started taking pictures.

Billy placed his hands against the window. "A few days after Janice's baby boy died, she found out her husband was killed in combat. She decided she couldn't live without them, so she ended her life; right here in this attic."

I yearned to reach for David but my feet were glued right where they were. I placed both hands on my stomach and exhaled.

"Janice won't hurt you, in fact, she's happy you're pregnant. She's been watching over you and praying your delivery goes well." He pauses. "It's hard for her to accept the fact that her husband and son are dead; it's especially hard for her to forgive herself for ending her own life. She's afraid she won't be welcomed into Heaven." Billy said.

The rocking chair moved faster, so fast that it nearly tipped over each time it swayed forward.

"This might be a good time for you to ask her to leave," Billy said.

"How do we do that?" I asked.

"It can be something simple, like please leave," he said.

David placed his hand on my shoulder. "Please leave," we said simultaneously. In fact, we chanted this until the rocking chair stilled.

Billy's eyes snapped open. "She's gone," he said. "I can't promise that she won't return but at least now you've asked her to move on."

"So what do we do now?" David asked.

"Continue on with your life."

"What if she comes back?" I asked.

"Then give me a call," Billy said. "If this doesn't work, there are other ways to remove ghosts from homes; I call 'it phase two.'"

Marissa and Billy silently gathered their tools. I wanted to ask more questions about Janice but all of a sudden I was exhausted. In fact, the experience felt like a drawn out panic attack.

After they left I asked David if he thought she was really gone.

"I hope so," he said.

***

The next two days turned into nights like clockwork. But on the third day, at seven am, my water broke.

"Oh my God, Sara, today's the day! Let's get you in the car and I'll bring out your suitcase."

"But I'm not due for another month and a half; those damn crazy pills must have caused this."

"Sweetie, if you hadn't taken the crazy pills, I would have started taking them."

"It's not time to make jokes, David."

"Regardless, he or she is ready." David's enthusiasm was contagious.

The next few hours alternated with periods of excitement, mainly from David, and periods of worry, mostly from me.

"Ten centimeters, it's time," the doctor said.

"It's in God's hands, Sara, and he's watching over you and our baby." David kissed me on the forehead.

"But it's too early!" I said.

"Push, Sara, push," the doctor said.

After what felt like eternity but was more likely a few minutes, our baby was born.

"It's a boy!" David said. "And he's perfect!"

After a few minutes, David laid our son on my chest. "It's nice to meet you, Aidan," I said. He was in fact, perfect.

David cocked his head. "Aidan? But I thought we decided on the name Cody."

"For some reason, he looks like an Aidan." I caressed his cheek. "Don't you like the name?"

"I do, I'm just surprised. What made you even think of that name?"

"I don't know…it just sort of popped in my head."

David leaned over and kissed me on the forehead. "Then Aidan it is."

Sometime after that, I fell asleep. When I woke, a slew of family and friends visited. At one point I noticed David was missing. "Where is he?" I asked his mother.

"He said he had a surprise for you."

When David returned, I was resting in the room alone. He handed me a bouquet of ruffled pink flowers.

"What are these?" I asked.

"Sweet peas, the April birth flower, but those are for Aidan." He placed them on the nightstand. Then he pulled a dozen red roses from behind his back. "These are for you."

"But you know, June 16th is my birthday, and not only is the rose my favorite flower, it is also the flower that represents June birthdays." I beamed.

"Birthday or not, I think you deserve them." He laughed.

Two evenings later, Aidan and I were released from the hospital. When we got home, Aidan and I settled in the rocking chair that I found at a local thrift shop. As we rocked back and forth, I noticed a wooden sign that read 'Aidan' hanging on the wall behind his crib.

"Here's your tea." David placed a mug on the lamp stand.

"David, where did that sign come from?"

"I found it in a box upstairs."

"What were you doing in the attic and why would there be a sign with our son's name on it?"

"I thought we would both feel better if the attic was cleaned out. While you were in the hospital, I moved everything to the Salvation Army. Betty and Jeff's other son must be named Aidan."

"Billy told us not to move anything, remember?" My voice sounded shrill. "Did you move the cross, too?"

"No, the cross is in a drawer in the curio cabinet. Sara, why don't you take a shower and relax."

The thought of a warm shower and a cup of tea sounded amazing, so I handed Aidan to David before heading into the bathroom. I stripped off my clothes and turned on the faucet. Remembering that my tea was in the nursery, I grabbed a towel and entered the hallway. I could hear David talking on the phone with someone. I didn't make a habit of eavesdropping on my husband but something in his voice sounded off. I paused in the hallway to listen.

"What? But that's bizarre!"

Who was he talking to? I peered around the corner. David was pacing back and forth across the kitchen.

"Thank you for your help, Mark. Goodbye."

I wrapped the towel tightly against my body and walked through the living room. "David, were you talking to Jeff and Betsy's son, Mark? Does he have a brother named Aidan?"

David's face was the color of chalk. "Yes, I was talking to Mark but his brother's name is Mike."

"Then who is named Aidan?"

"Janice's baby."

"No!" I dropped my towel and ran to the nursery. I breathed a sigh of relief when I found Aidan sleeping peacefully in his crib but as I was adjusting his blanket, I discovered the comfort cross next to him.

It was time for 'phase two.'

Kayanna Pepper

"Is *this* breakfast?" I ask Grandma as she layers a crock pot with chunks of carrot, celery, potato, onion, garlic and various spices including dried thyme and basil leaves.

My parents and I are spending Labor Day weekend at Grandma and Pap's farm house in southwestern Pennsylvania. It is so dang hot, however, that it feels like standing in line to ride Space Mountain at Disney World, right smack in the middle of the day. Pap says that the apocalypse is surely near for the sun to shine this bright in Pennsylvania.

The excess heat causes Grandma to sweat and every so often wipe her forehead and cheeks with the bottom of her apron. I am eager to escape the stifling house but Grandma will insist on breakfast first. I want to escape to the field with row after row of dry brown corn stalks which stand shriveled and exposed behind the barn.

As soon as I woke up, I peeked out the guest bedroom window which was covered in a thin film of dust. The clouds were cotton candy and the sun a giant sticky lemon lolly pop. Hydrangeas flourished in Grandma's garden. According to Grandma, hydrangeas symbolize 'heartfelt emotion' and these flowers make her happy.

She would probably be happier outside, too, especially if there's a slight breeze.

She laughs. "Of course not; this is our dinner."

"Then why are you making it so early?"

"It's nearly seven-thirty and this stew has to cook for nine hours."

"Oh, can I help?"

She nods. "Just let me cut the venison and then you can add the rest."

"What's venison?" I ask.

"Are you serious? Venison is deer meat and you've been eating it at my house since you were able to chew."

I place my hands around my neck and pretend to choke.

"Quit it; you're acting like your mother. I bet she doesn't cook much of anything, does she?"

"She does so, sometimes she makes spaghetti."

"A monkey could make spaghetti. If you lived closer, I'd give you cooking lessons every week." She pushes my sweaty brown bangs off to one side.

"Did you ever teach my mom how to cook?"

"I tried to but your mother wasn't interested." She takes a package wrapped in white paper out of the fridge with the word 'steks' written on it in blue marker.

"That's spelled wrong."

"Your Uncle Denny shot this deer and you know he can't spell all that well." After removing the white wrapper, Grandma pulls four pieces of black cherry colored meat from a bloody plastic bag and slices them into smaller chunks.

"I'm not eating *that*!"

"Now you sound as foolish as your mother and Julie." She sighs.

"Who's Julie?"

"She was my college roommate."

"I didn't know you went to college."

She winks. "There's a lot you don't know about your grandma."

"If you went to college, then how come you never worked anywhere?"

"My job was raising five children while tending a farm. Pour this beef broth into the pot and then add a healthy dose of black pepper."

"Did you ever dream of a job like Mom's?" My mother is a fashion designer for a well known company in New York City and my father is an editor for a popular magazine.

"In my heyday many girls went to college to find a husband. I suppose in a way, I did too. My ultimate dream was a family, period."

"Did Julie go to school to find a husband, too?"

"No, she was consumed by art, sculpting in particular. I'm not sure Julie could have ever loved a person the way she loved clay."

"Are you still friends?"

She grimaces. "Do you want to hear a story?"

"Yes!" I bounce up and down.

"Let me make your breakfast first. What'll it be? An omelet? Pancakes? Dippy eggs?"

"Mom told me to call them fried eggs, not dippy."

Grandma smirks. "Would you like fried eggs?"

I shake my head. "Cold cereal, please."

"Yuck." She places several boxes in front of me, along with a large bowl, spoon, and container of whole milk. "I only buy this crud because your pap has a sweet tooth." She sinks into the chair across from me. "Anyway, I lived in an off campus apartment during my senior year of college…"

"Where did you go to college?" I accidentally spit out a sugar puff.

Grandma hands me a napkin. "Can you just eat your cereal and listen?"

I hold a pointer finger to my lips and nod.

"I graduated from Pitt, its proper name is the University of Pittsburgh. Julie and I shared an off campus apartment a few blocks from school. We met as freshman in an art history class and our passion for art glued us together." She laughs. "Besides finding a husband and raising a family, I wanted to be an artist at that point."

I raise my hand like I do at school.

"Yes, Kayanna Pepper."

"Pepper is not my middle name. Why do you always call me that?"

"Your name reminds me of the hot red chili pepper. And you are in fact, spicy and feisty like a cayenne pepper, but if it bothers you, I'll stop."

"That's okay; I guess you can call me that. What kind of an artist did you want to be?"

"A painter."

"What did you like to paint?"

"Everything and anything really. Just smelling paint caused my heart to race."

"Why don't you paint anymore? You can still be an artist."

"That is a dream deferred. Anyway, back to the story. Even though Julie grew up in Philly and rooted against my Steelers, we were inseparable. She taught me how to play pool, I taught her how to sew, she taught me how to play poker, I taught her how to cook." Grandma pauses for a moment and her features harden like peach colored candle wax.

"The last meal that Julie and I prepared was venison stew. Julie chopped fresh vegetables and added spices but stopped when she noticed the package. It was wrapped in white paper but your Pap had prepared the package, so the word 'steak' was spelled correctly.

Pap and I were engaged by that time but I'm sure if he would have met Julie first, he would have fallen for her head over feet. It wasn't that she was particularly pretty… it was her aura. In fact, just being around Julie made a person feel special. Anyway, Julie asked, 'What kind of steak is that?' I explained that it was deer meat. 'Deer meat? Eww! I am not eating *that*,' she said. I asked if she had ever tasted it before. 'Well no, but I can't eat deer meat because it's too wild and gamey.' I explained how healthy venison was but she wouldn't hear of it."

"What makes it healthy?"

"I know that you've heard the expression, 'You are what you eat.' Well, deer eat acorns, apples, mushrooms, grasses, and grains. And when venison is prepared correctly, it's delicious."

"Did Julie try it?"

"No, she never did. She went on to say that deer are too pretty and gentle to hunt. Even after I explained that Pennsylvania was over populated with deer and if it weren't for hunters, the deer would starve to death, she said she couldn't eat Bambi's relatives.

It's a good thing she didn't grow up in my childhood home because your great grand pap was always toting deer, squirrel, rabbit and wild turkey home."

"Mom says she's a virgin and virgins don't eat meat."

"You mean 'vegan' not 'virgin.'" She shakes her head, smiling. "Your mother used to eat meat when she had sense. That New York City living brainwashed her. She just about forgot where she came from. But that's neither here nor there."

"What's Mom going to eat for dinner?"

"I'll fix her a salad and vegetable soup."

"Okay, then what happened in the story?"

"Julie and I walked the twelve blocks to our ten o'clock modern art class. Downtown Pittsburgh has plenty of steep hills and you can imagine how toned our legs were from hiking up and down hills each day. The morning was so beautiful that I nearly skipped class to paint the vast sky splattered with vanilla clouds and the yellow, orange and red leaves which decorated the trees like oversized sprinkles." She stared directly into my green eyes and continued. "I should have painted that day because it would have turned out amazing."

"So it's okay to skip school?"

"No, it's not okay to skip school, unless you're an artist. I'm just teasing you, Kayanna Pepper, you go to school. After class, Julie and I ate lunch at a little café called 'The Queen Bee.' Julie had her eye on a waiter named D J who played his guitar during work breaks. Your pap called the café 'artsy-fartsy.'"

I had to interrupt. "Did Pap go to college, too?"

"Yes, he earned his mechanical engineering degree. We were planning on staying in Pittsburgh, but then your great grand pap fell ill. In turn, we moved back to your pappy's hometown." She pauses to wipe her brow.

"After lunch, Julie and I headed back to campus for her sculpting and my drawing class. She gushed about D J the entire way and vowed to actually talk to him the next time we frequented the Queen Bee. He was the only one I knew of who caused her to blush and stammer. 'After class, want to take a drive through the country? I'd like to sketch for a while. Then we can hit McDonald's,' she said. 'I can't, Rob will be ready to eat a big bowl of stew once class lets out,' I said."

"I would have gone with Julie. Dad takes me to Mc Donald's on Thursdays after every tap class."

"Of course he does," she mutters.

"Is that the end of the story?"

"Not yet. As Julie drove through the town of Butler along winding country roads, a seven point whitetail deer dashed into the road, freezing at the sight of her Desoto Convertible. Julie loved that car and kept the top down well into late autumn. As usual, she wasn't wearing her seatbelt and when the car and deer collided, Julie was thrown from the convertible."

"Was she ok?"

"No, she wasn't. She died."

"Grandma, that's awful. Did the deer die, too?"

"Yes."

"You could have been with her!"

"For a long time I wished I would have been because losing Julie was like losing a sister. That's why I focused so much on raising a family with your grand pap. If you don't have family, you have nothing, Kayanna Pepper. Soon after her death, I graduated from Pitt, married your grand pap, and for the most part gave up painting. I did however paint a portrait of Julie which was on display at her funeral."

"Where's the picture of Julie now?"

"Her parents hung it above their mantel in their living room."

"Oh. Why'd you give up painting?"

"There just never seemed to be enough time. Your Uncle Denny was a handful with all of his issues, not to mention your mother and the other three."

"Don't you have time to paint now?"

"I suppose so."

"Then let's go buy art supplies."

"It's not that easy, kiddo."

"Why?"

"At the sight of a paint brush, I think of Julie."

"What's wrong with thinking about her?"

"It hurts my heart to think about her."

"I'm sorry, Grandma. I'll eat your stew."

"Good. In hindsight, we should have grilled hamburgers, hotdogs and vegetables for this evening. Oh well, now head outside and play."

I want to hug Grandma but she looks too hot so I leave her and her memories in the kitchen and eagerly sprint outside. The air is heavy with the sweet scent of her multicolor hydrangeas. We don't have a yard in the city but we do have a brick courtyard with wrought iron benches, a chipped porcelain fountain where pigeons bathe, and a single olive tree which must be wrapped each winter.

While I wander the corn field, I yearn for a brother or a sister but I know my parents barely want me let alone another kid. If I had a sibling, we could play hide and seek behind the ten foot corn stalks. There are plenty of cousins but they live even further away than New York City and I usually only see them at weddings and funerals. Uncle Denny lives near Grandma and Pap's house but he doesn't have children which my mother says is a blessing.

I wish for company but Denny and Pap took a drive to Carlisle to check out a tractor, and they aren't expected back until dinner. Meanwhile Mom and Dad are sleeping their life away, and Grandma is consumed with cooking and cleaning.

I soon grow tired of the naked corn field and head into the weathered barn which seems to grow wrinkles each year like Grandma. When my mom was little, she played with goats, chickens, rabbits, cats and dogs. At one time she even had a llama. Presently a few stray cats reside in the barn but they eye me warily with their yellow eyes. I nestle into a mound of hay and contemplate things to do. I could splash in the shallow creek, spin on the tattered tire swing, shop at the clearance store...that's what I'll do. I'll surprise Grandma with art supplies!

I creep into the house and up the stairs to the guest room where my parents sleep. I perch on the edge of the bed and gently shake my father's shoulders. "Daddy, daddy," I whisper. He's wearing boxer briefs and my mom is dressed in underwear and a tank top. There are several rickety fans facing the bed but they're barely blowing any air.

"What?" He mutters while opening his eyelids half way.

"Daddy, can I have some money to go to the clearance store?"

"Sure, take as much as you need from my wallet. I think it's on the dresser top."

My mother mumbles, "What time is it?"

"It's ten o'clock. Want to go to the store with me?"

"I'm so hot that I don't have the energy to get out of bed," she says.

"Okay, well I'll see you later. Thanks, Daddy." I pull a wad of cash from his wallet.

I tiptoe down the stairs, through the kitchen, sun porch, and finally to the gravel road that is so hot you could fry an entire southern breakfast.

After skipping along the road for like fifteen minutes, I finally see Mrs. Sampson's house. Max, her coal black dachshund puppy, barely lifts his head from the porch floor. Even the daisy petals droop and the butterflies which usually dance among these showy flowers hover lazily.

Mr. Miller is Mrs. Sampson's closest neighbor, which is still pretty far away. As usual Mr. Miller is wearing jean overalls without a shirt. He waves a half-hearted hello as he refills multiple bird feeders.

"Good morning, Mr. Miller," I holler.

"How are younz doin'?" He hollers back.

"Just fine. How about younz guys?"

"Can't complain about much, except for this heat."

My mother says that my dialect changes to hick whenever we visit Grandma and Pap. I'm not sure exactly what hick means but from her tone I assume it's unacceptable. Daddy always tells her that she's too hard on me.

About five minutes later, I reach the Larson's place. Jake and Julia Larson take turns barreling down an orange and blue slide into a plastic pool. I smile as they shriek and splash, and briefly consider joining them, but I'm on a mission. Besides, they're little kids.

"Hi, Kayanna," they say.

By the time I reach the clearance store, my green cotton tank top, jean shorts and hair are drenched in sweat. I welcome the slightly cooler atmosphere as I enter the vast store; the bell diligently announces my arrival.

"Can I help you find something?" Mrs. James asks before lifting her head from a well worn fashion magazine which is resting on a locked glass counter filled with cigarette lighters and pipes like my Uncle Denny uses. A handmade sign reads 'For Use With Tobacco Products Only!'"

"Hi, Mrs. James."

"Kayanna, it's nice to see you. I'd give you a hug if it weren't so muggy. Looking for anything in particular?"

"No." I fib because I look forward to browsing the entire clearance shop in all its random glory.

"Well, holler if you need anything. Everything is ten percent off for you, dear."

"Thanks." I grab a metal shopping basket. I venture through the lanes and fiddle with a Mardi Gras necklace with large purple, gold, and green beads. I contemplate purchasing a container of gold fish food because Daddy keeps promising to take me to a pet store but never gets around to it. I notice that the sugary gummy candy appears sticky and unappetizing. I wonder who would buy Pittsburgh Steelers calendars from years past, gaudy knick knacks, or oversized underwear. I place a large bottle of bubbles into my empty shopping basket.

Lane ten is the only one which holds my interest. I bypass lined notebook paper, business envelopes and Scotch tape. I carefully examine the limited art supplies and before long the bubbles share the basket with a plastic set of watercolors, multi-color construction paper, pre-sharpened pencils, markers, and finger paint.

Satisfied, I make my way to the cash register where Mrs. James fans her face with the fashion magazine. "Well aren't you the little Monet." She rings up the purchases.

"Actually everything except the bubbles is for my grandma. She used to paint and I want to help her paint again."

"I didn't know Stella was artistic. That's very nice of you."

"Am I the only customer?"

"Afraid so. Folks are busy with church and family dinners on Sundays. There's just not enough traffic to stay open seven days a week. In fact today will be the last Sunday we're open."

"My grandparents go to church on Saturday evenings. I'm glad you were open today."

"Take care of yourself, Kayanna."

"Thank you, Mrs. James."

***

When I return to Grandma's, I stash my purchases in the guest closet. In the living room, Grandma is watching a movie on the Lifetime channel and my parents are consumed with their lap tops.

"Boy do you look hot, Kayanna. You better take a cool shower," my father says.

"And drink some iced tea. I'll get it for you." Grandma shuffles into the kitchen.

"Those are pretty dresses. " I peer over my mother's shoulder.

"Why thank you, love. These are Stella Lilly originals." Stella Lilly is the name of my mother's fashion line. Stella is my grandma's name and Lilly is my mother's.

I chug the iced tea that Grandma hands me before taking the coldest shower possible. Afterward I change into a pretty purple sun dress because I know how much it will please my mother.

Fortunately by dinner time, Mother Nature is in a compassionate mood, for the sun's rays recede and the temperature feels more like a soothing bath than an oven. We decide to transport dinner to the faded picnic tables underneath the pavilion. Besides the venison stew, Grandma made potato and pasta salad, deviled eggs, hard boiled eggs soaked in beet juice, iced tea, a salad and vegetable soup for my mother, and mini chocolate gob cakes. Grandma says gobs, which are cakes with icing on the inside, instead of on the outside, originated in medieval Germany.

I light the citronella candles before handing out Styrofoam plates, napkins, and plastic utensils. I sit between my parents and Uncle Denny sits between his. Pap says grace before I dig into the stew.

"Your stew is delicious, Grandma," I say.

"Thank you, dear." She winks at me.

I drink iced tea while everyone else, even Grandma, drink cans of Coors Light. After a few beers, Dad says that Mom sounds like a hick which makes everyone laugh.

After dinner, the boys play cards at the picnic table and the girls climb onto the wooden swing. I relax against my mother's shoulder and breathe in her scent of tart green apples. She strokes my hair which makes my eyes heavy but I am desperate to remain awake.

"When are you coming back?" Grandma asks.

"Mom, we're still here. Why do you worry when we're visiting next when we're here?" My mother laughs.

"I enjoy Kayanna's company and look forward to her visits." Grandma grins.

***

I must have dozed off because the next thing I remember is lying limp like a rag doll in Daddy's arms. The purple tinted sky envelops us as the stars guide us through the lush yard which reminds me of a jungle that I read about in a story book.

I perk up after changing into a light cotton night gown, washing my face, and brushing my teeth with cool water. I clutch the plastic bag full of gifts for Grandma as I sneak up behind her in the kitchen, as she places leftovers in Tupperware containers.

"I have something for you, Grandma."

After placing a container into the fridge, she turns to face me with a puzzled expression.

"Here." I thrust the bag at her.

Grandma slowly removes and examines each item before carefully placing them on the kitchen table.

"Maybe the paint will make your heart race and you'll be an artist again."

She embraces me in her strong golden arms. "I love you so much, Kayanna Pepper."

"I love you, too, Grandma."

We stand still for several moments before she suggests that I go to sleep.

***

The next morning, I wipe away the dust from the guest bedroom window before glancing out at Grandma and Pap's world. Once again the lemon yellow sun warms the earth and sky and bags of white cotton candy hang among faded stars.

Then I notice Grandma surrounded by hydrangeas, her easel propped in front of her. I can't tell if she's drawing or painting, but either way, a serene smile lights up her face.

"Oh my gosh," I whisper. I notice a white tailed deer watching Grandma. She slowly tilts her head toward the deer and they gaze at one another for a moment before the deer dashes into the cornfield. My grandmother closes her eyes and tilts her head as if in prayer. Then she picks up either a pencil or a thin paint brush and becomes an artist.

Even In Death

Present

My knees sink into the red Virginia clay beside Amy's grave. Usually I prop a pack of Kools against her headstone, but this morning, I feel slightly creative. I slice open the pack and pull out ten cigarettes. I arrange the white sticks so they spell out her name. Then I gaze at the AMY cigarette art and as usual, wait for her.

"Hi, Mark," says my favorite undertaker. He's leaning out the window of his rusty pick up truck.

"Morning, Billy."

"Cold enough for you?" Billy is a man of few words but he enjoys bullshitting about the weather.

"It could always be colder, I suppose."

"Ain't that the truth? See you later." The truck kicks up dust and gravel.

As far as I can tell, there are no other live guests at the Columbia Gardens Cemetery because if there were, I'd be hounded.

"Really, Mark? The sun hasn't woken and you're already here." Amy's spirit rises casually from the earth. She leans her back against the headstone and hugs her knees against her chest.

"Nice touch." She motions to the cigarette arrangement before plucking one. "Got a light?"

"Of course." I lean in closer to light her cigarette as I've done countless times before. She closes her jet black eyes, purses her lips, and inhales. Even in death, Amy is beautiful. Even in death, she's not a morning person.

Her eyes open lazily like a stoned teenager. "Why so early?"

"Business has really taken off. From now on I'm afraid my visits will either be before sunrise or after sunset."

She juts out her chin and pouts as if she were seven-years-old instead of twenty-seven. Forever twenty-seven.

"Amy." I sigh. "You understand, don't you?"

She flicks the cigarette butt, hitting an oak tree. "When I died, things stopped making sense, Mark."

***

Past

Amy died two years ago on a Tuesday evening in November. Earlier that day, she was waiting for me directly in front of the Ballston metro. As usual, she seemed oblivious to the people swarming like wasps around her. She was wearing a grey pea coat which matched the sky's mood. She was puffing on a cigarette and tapping her black boot in time to the loud music blaring from her IPOD. It was either the alternative rock band Evanescence or the metal band Lacuna Coil; I could never differentiate the two. I snuck up behind her, wrapped my arms around her tiny waist, and lifted her off the ground. She shrieked and kicked her legs until I released her. She spun around and clenched her fists before she realized it was me.

"Are you trying to give me a heart attack?" Beaming, she flung her arms around my neck and pulled me close. Her jet black hair smelled of course like cigarettes but also of lavender; my favorite flower. When Amy stepped back, I noticed a few purple streaks outlining her face.

"When did you do that?" I asked.

"You like? During my lunch break. Leigh helped."

"I do like."

She smirked. "Good because it's permanent."

"Why does that not surprise me?" I laced my fingers through hers as we waited to cross the street. Her fingers felt cold and her nose was slightly pink. She was beautiful but not in a girls-next-door-kind of way. When Amy and I first met, I described her to my friends as, 'More like Angelina Jolie, less like Jennifer Aniston.'"

When we reached Wilson Boulevard, I asked if she wanted to grab dinner and drinks at Rock Bottom.

"Of course I do. It's trivia night!"

We shared Ball Park pretzels with spinach dip, Mini Street tacos, and of course a few I.P.A. ales. Amy kicked my ass at trivia. At ten o'clock, Amy yawned.

"And I'm supposed to be the night owl," she said.

As I was putting on my jacket, my hand brushed a little box which had been traveling with me for a few weeks. It wasn't that I was indecisive. In fact, when I met Amy, my first thought was; 'I wish we would have met sooner.' Because I knew that even with the future laid out like a red carpet, there would never be enough time with her.

I just couldn't think of any proposal that was unique enough for Amy. She was the creative one; hair stylist by day, painter by night. I was an accountant who couldn't draw stick figures straight. And yet Amy loved me anyway.

When we left the restaurant, we were hit with a blast of cold air. Amy's teeth chattered. "Can you believe its winter already? Where does the time go?"

"Screw it." I pulled the ring box from my pocket.

"Screw wh-"Amy stopped mid-sentence as I knelt in front of her.

"Amy Elizabeth Parker, you are the most exquisite woman I have ever met in my life. And you are the woman I want to spend the rest of my life and afterlife with. Will you marry me?"

"Yes!" She squealed and jumped up and down before she offered her left hand. I slipped the ruby ring onto her finger. "Mark, it's gorgeous." She knelt down beside me and kissed me hard on the lips.

I didn't know that would be the last time we ever kissed.

We hugged each other so tightly we had trouble breathing and when we let go, we laughed. I stood, helped her up, and clasped her left hand; enjoying the way the ring pressed against my palm. The walk light flashed and we stepped into the crosswalk. The bright lights from the black Escalade shined over us, like a harsh wave pounding against the shore. It was the strangest thing- to be kissing on the street corner one minute, and laying on stretchers the next. It felt like a poorly written action flick except that the main actress didn't survive; the white sheet remained.

Even though my counselor says that it's an irrational belief, I blame myself. No, I wasn't the drunk elderly driver; and no, I'm not a fortune teller; but even so, I was the one who proposed on a street corner, for Christ's sake! If I had only been more creative, perhaps Amy would still be alive. Perhaps she'd be my wife.

Doctors say it was a miracle I survived. I say it's a curse.

***

Present

"I'm sorry I've been acting like such a shit," Amy says. "It's just hard seeing you move on without me."

"But Amy, I'm not moving on. I'm merely existing. Do you know how often I contemplate jumping in front of the metro? Every single day."

"I'm sorry." She places her hand on my shoulder but I don't feel it. We haven't figured out why she's able to hold objects but not people. It's cruel to be able to see but not touch each other.

"Helping people is the only thing that keeps me going. Well, that and seeing a shrink twice a month."

A ghost tear slips down Amy's cheek.

"Bertha, isn't that the fellow that communicates with the dead? Maybe he can speak to Harry." I look up to find two elderly women ogling me.

Behind them, a redheaded woman emerges. "Don't bother. He's a fake." Her icy blue eyes narrow.

"Then who's he talking to?" One of the women asks her.

"If I had to guess? Satan," she replies.

The elderly women gasp and shuffle away.

"What a nut job." Amy sighs. "You better go. Goodbye for today, Mark."

"I'll be back soon, baby. Goodbye for today, Amy."

***

Past

Before the accident, I had zero supernatural abilities. And unlike Amy, I didn't believe in horoscopes, or psychics, or anything out of the realm of normalcy. But then on the one year anniversary of Amy's death, that all changed. I had spent the entire day slouching on a bench near her grave. Her parents were serving dinner at their home for all of Amy's friends but I felt compelled to remain right where I was.

Leigh, Amy's coworker that I never liked, tried to persuade me to attend the dinner. "Don't you want to uh, remember Amy by like sharing memories of her life?" She resembled a mouse with blonde hair and a nose ring. As usual she looked as high as Amy Winehouse in her heyday.

"Believe me, every memory of Amy is forever etched in my heart. I don't need to talk to people who thought they knew her, but really didn't," I snapped.

Before I could apologize, she scurried away.

At eight o'clock, when the cemetery technically closed, I rested against Amy's headstone and shivered. When it got so cold that my fingers stung, I buried my hands in my coat pockets. In my right pocket, I found a pack of Kools. On a whim, I had bought them that morning at a gas station. Not for me, for Amy. I placed the pack among yellow carnation flowers tied with hot pink ribbon, oversized teddy bears that looked like carnival game prizes, and other ridiculous things people brought. Clearly they didn't know Amy very well. She never wanted flowers because her cat Pollock used to desecrate them. And any stuffed animal instantly became a chew toy for her dog, Warhol.

"What the hell." I mumbled as I lifted a cigarette from the pack. I lit it and took a small puff. I immediately started coughing.

"Easy tiger, those things will kill you." Amy's spirit was floating next to me, whispering in my ear.

"Amy!

"You can see me?" Her eyes grew round. "How?"

"I don't know. Baby, is it really you?" I reached out to touch her cheek but all I felt was air. That's when my eyes filled with tears.

"It's really me. Mark, I've been trying to communicate with you from day one. Why can you see me now, all of a sudden?"

"Is it because this is the day that…" I didn't want to say it.

She nodded. "That must be it."

"Baby, I miss you so much." Again, I tried to touch her.

In response, Amy cried so hard her body shook.

I tried to wrap my arms around her to no avail. "God, Amy, it's not fair! I should be lying next to you." I point to the soft earth.

She plucked the cigarette and lighter from my fingers. "If you keep smoking these, you just might be. But they won't harm me anymore, will they?" She puffed away.

My lips formed a small smile.

The next four hours passed quickly. Suffice it to say, I had a lot of questions.

"What's it like? The afterlife, I mean."

She tilted her face to the sky. "It's paradise and yet it's not home. Like the time we vacationed in Cancun but missed Arlington." She dropped her head. She picked up dirt and crumbled it between her fingers. "Does that make sense?"

"Yes, it does."

"Speaking of home, how are my mom and dad? How's Scott?"

"They miss you, of course. But they're doing as well as can be expected."

She bobbed her head like a pigeon. "Will you look after them?"

"I still have dinner with them every Sunday."

Amy's smile lit up her face. "I knew you were a keeper."

For a moment we don't speak but it's a comfortable silence, the kind you can only have with someone who knows you inside and out. It reminded me of the time I went skydiving and had five glorious minutes of complete silence. Most people prefer the one minute free fall- the whoosh of air screaming in your ears- but not me. How amazing it would be to skydive at night among the stars, light years away from the Earth. I gazed at the sky but it was hard to see the stars through the canopy of oak trees.

Amy glanced at my cell phone. "Mark, its well after midnight..."

"And I can still see you." I tried to kiss her but my lips met only air.

I stayed with her until dawn and only left because Amy noticed that my lips were blue.

"Goodbye for today, Mark."

"Goodbye for today, Amy. I'll see you soon." I prayed this was true.

I came back the next day but Amy didn't appear. At least I couldn't see her. After two weeks straight, I was convinced I wouldn't see her until next November, on the second anniversary of her death. I slumped against her grave. I thought about giving up on life because life without Amy was shit. I shoved my hands in my pockets and discovered a crumpled pack of cigarettes. I pulled them out and propped them against the head stone. The next thing I knew, Amy's spirit was beside me.

"Oh my God, baby, I see you!" I tried to cup her dainty chin with my clumsy hand.

"Those must be magical freakin' cigarettes." She laughed.

***

One evening, on my way out of the cemetery, undertaker Billy approached me as if I were a caged lion. "Are you doing okay, Mark?"

"Yes, I'm actually feeling better than I have in a long time. What about you?"

"I'm good. It's just that I'm uh, worried about you. I uh, noticed that you've been talking to yourself a lot lately and uh..."

"Actually, I've been talking to Amy." I'm relieved to tell someone. I haven't mentioned it to anyone else for fear they'd have me committed. For some reason, I trust Billy wouldn't do that. But if he tried to, I could deny saying anything of the sort.

Billy ran a hand through his shaggy blonde hair. "I uh, don't know what to say."

"Are you off the clock?"

"Yeah."

"Let's go for a beer. I'll explain everything."

The next evening, Billy and I were standing in front of William Reinhart's grave. Billy clutched a bottle of Jack Daniels and two shot glasses.

"This might not work, Billy, so I apologize in advance."

"All I ask is that you try."

"You ready?"

"Hell yes." His hands shook so badly I had to fill the shot glasses for him. I set one on the gravestone and handed Billy the other. He threw it back quickly.

"Now what do we do?" He asked.

"We wait."

Billy placed his hands on his hips and stared at the grave.

A watched clock never tells the time, I thought.

But after a few minutes, a tall, wiry man's shadow appeared.

"Can you see him?" I asked.

"No. Can you?"

I nod. "Mr. Reinhart?"

He grinned. "Please call me Bubba."

"What's he saying?" Billy's voice quivered.

"He asked me to call him Bubba."

"Oh my God, Dad, you're really here!"

***

Afterwards, Billy asked if I could help his friend Melissa, whose mother had passed away a few months ago. I agreed to meet her at the cemetery.

"Hi, Mark. I'm Melissa." She offered her hand and we shook.

"Hi. I can't promise this will work but what object did your mother most identify with?"

She scrunched her freckled nose. "Well, she loved to crochet but she also loved riding her horse." She pulled a ball of green yarn and a hook from her bag. I instructed her to place the items next to the headstone. Nothing happened.

"Do you have a picture of her horse?"

"I do." Melissa opened her wallet and pulled out a picture of her mother next to a handsome white stallion. "His name is Jones." She propped the picture against the headstone but again nothing happened.

"Could you bring Jones here? I'm sure Billy could help smuggle him in."

"It's worth a shot, isn't it? Does nine o'clock tomorrow morning work?"

I checked the calendar on my phone. "No problem."

The next morning Melissa led Jones to her mother's grave. Like clockwork, Marjorie's spirit materialized and mother and daughter had a lengthy conversation via me.

Following the visit, Melissa asked if she could interview me for the local newspaper. I was hesitant but felt fulfilled by helping her and Billy, so I agreed. After the article came out, I was bombarded with requests; so many that I quit my accounting job. I made considerably less money but felt intrinsically richer.

The redheaded woman read about me in the newspaper.

***

Present

I'm sleeping blissfully when the door bell wakes me. The clock reads forty minutes after midnight. I lug myself to the front door and peer through the peep hole. Shit. I brace myself before I open the door.

"How can you do this to people? You're a fake!" The redheaded woman's pretty face is twisted. She slips past me and stands in the middle of my living room.

Instead of asking what the hell she's doing at my house in the middle of the night, I ask her if she would like a cup of tea or coffee.

"Tea would be nice."

I nod and she follows me into the kitchen.

"Please have a seat." I motion to a stainless steel stool.

As I prepare two cups of tea, she's silent. Perhaps she's contemplating killing me. I can't help but think about her girl-next-door beauty. Like Jennifer Aniston, less like Angelina Jolie.

***

Past

Three months ago, she approached me in the cemetery. She had recently buried her five-year-old son and was desperate to make contact. However, she wished to remain anonymous. In fact, she covered her son's headstone with a bed sheet the few times we attempted to communicate with him. The first time she brought a football. The second, a toy truck. The third, a teddy bear. Nothing worked. And according to her, it was my fault. She's borderline stalked me since.

***

Present

"Here." I place a cup of English breakfast tea in front of her. She takes a sip of tea before saying, "I have a pistol." She motions to the purse on her lap.

"Are you going to use it?"

"I don't know." She sobs and for some reason her tears remind me of melting icicles.

For all of my talk about jumping in front of a Metro, I'm shaken. Should I tackle her? Instead I sit down on the stool beside her.

"I'm not going to kill you." She pauses to wipe her eyes with the sleeve of her white sweatshirt, before she reaches in her purse for the pistol. "But I might kill myself."

"That won't bring him back," I say quietly.

"I know why he isn't coming."

"Why's that?" I expect her to say that his favorite gift is a lost Matchbox car, or something along those lines.

"Because I killed him." She gets up from the stool, pacing back and forth across the kitchen, all the while clutching the pistol. I should have tackled her when I had the chance.

"What happened?"

"A nurse at the hospital called off at the last minute and it was my turn to cover. It was late, after eight o'clock, and I thought Josh was inside with my husband, who's now my ex-husband. But he was still outside, riding his bicycle. I didn't see him, just heard the awful crunch of his bicycle when I ran over it!" Sobs rack her body.

"Please give me the gun." I expect a struggle but she hands it to me. It's not loaded. I drop it on the counter before placing a hand on her shoulder.

"What's your name?"

"Cora."

We talk for hours about Amy and Josh until sleep takes hold. Cora collapses on the couch and I return to bed. Again, I can't help but think how beautiful Cora is. Beautiful yet broken like pieces of fine china trapped on the Titanic.

In the morning Cora asks if I'll meet her at the cemetery.

"Only if you promise to make an appointment with a grief counselor. You need to talk to a professional that can help you."

"I promise to find a counselor. I'll bring Josh's bicycle." She hangs her head. "That was his favorite toy." I reach for her and she sinks into my arms. She smells like oranges, my favorite fruit.

Before meeting with Cora, I purchase a carton of cigarettes at the corner gas station. Then I visit Amy's grave. Using several packs of cigarettes, I spell out: "Even In Death, I Love You Amy." But before she rises, I walk away.

EVEN IN DEATH

Motivator

I have a thirty-year-old secret. This secret consumes me as I pass a serving bowl of cranberry sauce to my ninety-seven-year-old grandfather.

"I don't eat this can crap," he says.

My mother replies, "Dad, please don't."

"Don't what?"

"Don't be difficult." She sighs.

"I'm old so I've earned the right to act any damn way I please." He winks. He's got a point. He thoroughly enjoys teasing my mother because she always has a reaction.

"This turkey's dry," he says. He's got another good point. My mother ignores him for once. I'm sure he's also thinking that the gravy is cold and lumpy, the rolls are doughy and the imminent pumpkin pie will be bland. My mother chooses quantity over quality like public school lunch ladies. My parents have five children; therefore, her shabby cooking is understandable.

My father pours grandpa a glass of brandy. "That's more like it." Grandpa takes a long swig.

Grandpa is my favorite part of family dinner, whereas he irritates my nearly identical twin sister, Annabelle; and at times, my mother.

Annabelle is a motivational speaker and somewhat of a celebrity. Her picture is plastered on mugs, calendars, hats, tee shirts, and other trinkets that people actually purchase. But it's not only her face, it's mine.

After eating a piece of pumpkin pie which is tolerable with extra whipped cream, my mother says, "Ericka, Annabelle, please clear the table. I have to take Grandpa back." Grandpa stands next to the door, clutching his walker and wearing an old fashion suit jacket and fedora. Grandpa never verbalizes when he wants to leave; he simply stands by the door like Bruno, our family bulldog, does when he needs to pee.

"Bye Grandpa." I hug him gently.

"Goodbye Grandfather," Annabelle calls from the dining room.

"There's something not right about that one," Grandpa mutters.

"Why do you say that?" I ask.

Before he can respond my mother is ushering him out the door. "Don't worry, Dad, I'll get you back in time for movie night. They're showing *It's a Wonderful Life*. Maybe they'll serve wine and cheese."

"They serve popcorn on movie night, Elizabeth, not wine and cheese. Anyway, the wine and cheese tasting was a joke. We had to pick between a Dixie cup of white and a Dixie cup of red. I'm near one hundred years old, for Christ's sake but they wouldn't let me taste both. And they handed out unsalted crackers and orange square cheese wrapped in plastic..." His voice trails off as they slowly make their way down the driveway.

"C'mon, slacker," Annabelle hollers from the kitchen. I gather water glasses from the table. I'm tired from the dry turkey and would prefer to join my father in the living room, especially since the Redskins are playing the Eagles.

Annabelle is shoving plates into the dishwasher while Bruno whines at the door.

"Shut up, Bruno," she says.

My secret is that I'd like to shut Annabelle up in a hospital for awhile. I don't want to kill her, but I do want her to feel pain.

***

Twenty years ago, Annabelle heard me reciting Pocahontas' lines for our fifth grade Thanksgiving play.

"You can't be Pocahontas." Her hands were on her hips and she was scowling.

"Why not? I know all of the lines by heart."

"Because you'll freeze up like a cherry popsicle on stage. Your face always turns bright red and you stutter and," she paused dramatically, "you have that spot on your face."

I stuck my tongue out at her as she skipped out of our bedroom. I touched my forehead and although I couldn't feel anything, I knew and always will know that my birthmark is there.

The next day she asked Mrs. Malone for a copy of Pocahontas's lines.

She got the part.

***

I reluctantly join Annabelle in the kitchen.

"I mean it Bruno, shut up," she says.

"Why don't you open the door and let him out instead of telling him to shut up?"

"I'm busy." She dumps mashed potatoes down the garbage disposal.

I open the door for Bruno and he dashes out into the achingly cold night. "I'm sure Mom wants to save the leftover food." I pour carrots into a plastic container.

"Leftover food is disgusting." She turns on the disposal. I could shove her arm into the disposal but that would be too gruesome.

"I bet Grandpa's dead before Christmas." She says this as nonchalantly as a weather reporter whose only news is that the day is 'clear and sunny.'"

"What an awful thing to say."

"Oh, like you don't wonder when the old miser is going to kick the bucket. I also wonder how much money he has stashed under his mattress. Then again, the nursing home staff probably got to it first."

"That's sick." I shudder.

"I was just kidding. Lighten up, Pollyanna." She rolls her eyes.

I fondle a large carving knife but think better of using it. I rinse off the knife and hand it to her with the tip pointing towards her but she doesn't notice. She just simply plucks it from my hands and drops it in the dishwasher.

"So how's life counseling preteens?" She knows this is a touchy subject.

"They've been squirrelly lately but that's normal around the holidays."

"So when are you going to shit or get off of the pot?"

"I don't mind my job all that much."

"Liar, I know your dream is to be a writer." She enunciates the word writer.

"I am a writer."

"I mean a published author." She smirks.

"If I had to rely on you for motivation, I'd stick my head in an oven," I say. Actually I'd like to shove her head in an oven.

"It's called tough love, baby, and my clients love it. And you don't even take advantage of the fact that my motivation is free to you."

"Your kind of motivation has the opposite effect on me." She laughs, assuming I'm joking. I need some fresh air. I dry my hands off with a dishtowel with dancing chili peppers all over it before heading to the back porch. Bruno is whining to come in while I am hungering to get out.

***

"What took you so long?" My father asks as my mother flings open the door bringing in a gust of harsh wind.

"It's snowing," she says. Her cheeks are flushed and her hair is disheveled.

"How are the tires holding up?" He asks.

"They're just fine, honey."

Rigging Annabelle's car is too risky. Suppose she crashes and dies? And I don't know the first thing about cars. Carbon monoxide poisoning? But she doesn't even have a garage, so that's a ridiculous idea.

"Who's winning?" My mother asks.

"We're up seven." He grins.

"Go Skins." My mother pumps her fist. "Does anyone want a cup of coffee?"

The three of us say a simultaneous 'yes.' I follow her into the kitchen.

"Grandpa's doing well, right?" I ask.

"As well as can be expected but who knows if he'll make it to Christmas."

"I'll make sure to visit him this week."

"He'll like that." She dumps a heaping portion of cheap coffee grains into the filter.

Annabelle enters the kitchen. "Please don't add cream to my coffee. I think I may be lactose intolerant."

"Since when?" Our mother asks.

"Since forever I think." I could make her sick but with what? Unfortunately she isn't allergic to anything; she's only claiming a potential milk allergy for attention. In the past she was certain she was allergic to gluten and strawberries, but it turned out to be excessive gas. If only she had a peanut or shellfish allergy, especially peanuts because you can shove those suckers into anything. There is a table in the cafeteria at the middle school where I work that is specifically for kids with food allergies. There are stickers plastered on the table with 'Don't Feed Me!' and 'Peanut Allergy!'

"I can't stay too late because I have a speaking engagement in the early morning. It's in D.C. of course. I have to go home and take a bath, choose my outfit…" I could toss a space heater into the tub but then I'd electrocute her.

"I'm so proud of you, Annabelle. You've become such a success," our mother says.

"Aren't you proud of Ericka too?"

"Of course I am. I'm proud of all five of my wonderful children. It's too bad that your brothers couldn't make the trip."

***

The following Tuesday, I pull into a parking space directly in front of the Belfont Nursing Home. The surrounding trees are white and withered; a precursor to the prisoners within held captive by time.

There is a stillness to Belfont; a certain stagnation similar to a fishing pond that my father used to drag us to when we were little.

I sign the guest book before turning right. Belfont has been newly renovated and resembles a hotel more so than a rest stop before death. But even though the hardwood floors are shiny and the TV's are massive and the couches actually look comfortable; there is an intrinsic stillness to Belfont that no amount of decoration or activity can shake.

Annabelle refuses to visit Grandpa because elderly people supposedly scare her. I admit, sometimes they make me uncomfortable because they appear fragile like baby birds without mothers. However, my grandfather lives here, my only remaining grandparent, so I built a bridge and got over it. That's what my grandma used to say.

I loudly rap on his door before opening it. Grandpa is lying in bed although it is a little after five o'clock.

"Hello Grandfather, its Ericka." I place a poinsettia plant and a plate of cookies on the small kitchen table.

"Why hello." He slowly sits up and fumbles for his walker. As he makes his way to the recliner, I remove my scarf, mittens, and coat.

"What kind of cookies did you bring?"

"Your favorite, ginger and molasses. Would you like them now with some milk?"

"That sounds good."

I pull out a carton of milk from the miniature refrigerator. Grandpa's apartment is actually quite nice with a little kitchen, bathroom, bedroom, and living area.

"Here you go." I place the cookies and milk on a tray.

Then I notice several recent photos hanging on the wall. "Those are nice pictures."

"Your mother put those up," he says, although it sounds like 'your muver put wose up,' since his mouth is full of cookie.

Photos of ghosts are haunting the photos of the living; I think as I glance at a picture of my grandmother, two of my aunts and my uncle. Three out of five of my grandfather's children and his wife are dead. There is something inherently wrong about burying your children.

He points to a recent photo. "Your father's gained some weight but it can't be because of your mother's cooking. It's probably due to your delicious cookies."

"Thank you. I guess that's my one talent."

"You know your grandmother was a very talented artist," he says. Three of her miniature paintings hang on the wall. They are vibrant and shiny and alive.

"I miss her," I say.

"Me, too. Is that you or your sister in that picture?" He points to a picture of Annabelle leaning against a cherry blossom tree in Washington, D.C.

"That's Annabelle."

"There's something wrong with that one."

"Why do you say that?"

"Remember I'm old. I've met a lot of people in my time and I recognize when someone is *off.*"

"Grandpa, can I tell you a secret that I've never told anyone?"

"I'll take it to my grave and beyond."

I take a deep breath. "I don't love or even like her."

"Who?" Grandpa's forehead wrinkles even more.

"Annabelle. Sometimes I feel like I hate her."

"Hate is a very strong word, Ericka. The only time I have ever truly hated anyone was during war. If you didn't hate the enemies, then how could you find it in your heart to kill them?"

"Annabelle is like an enemy but I don't want to kill her, just hurt her," I say.

"Then you need to take out the enemy," he says. He looks so tired and worn out; it is clearly time for me to go.

"I'll let you rest." I rise and place a kiss on his forehead.

"You're a good girl, Ericka." He pats my back.

***

As I drive home through the icy streets my grandfather's words run circles around my mind like gerbils glued to a wheel. Did he just encourage me to kill Annabelle, his own granddaughter? He was ninety-seven years old, so clearly he wasn't all there, was he?

***

"Hello." My sister answers the phone as if my calling was right up there with attending mass, which she loathes. Annabelle is one of those people who will call you while she's driving and then as soon as she reaches her destination, she will have to go, even if you're in mid-sentence. As if the person on the other line is an afterthought or filler that you can scrape off, like excess cream cheese on a bagel.

"Hi, what are you up to?" I try to sound casual.

"I'm heading out the door, what's up?"

"I was wondering if you'd like to meet up for dinner one night this week."

"What's the occasion? It can't be your birthday because I'd never forget that." She laughs.

"Maybe you can check out one of my short stories and tell me what you think." I say the first thing that pops in my head and instantly regret it.

"I knew you wanted something from me, why else would you call? The only night that I'm free is Thursday."

"That works for me," I say quickly.

"Where shall we meet?"

"I'll come to your place first. Maybe you can read the story there before we go to dinner."

"That's fine. I have an extra bottle of an amazing Pinot Noir that one of my clients brought back from Canada. We'll have a few cocktails before dinner."

"Does seven work?"

"Seven is perfect, see you then." She hangs up before I have the chance to say goodbye.

***

I decide on a simple gray dress with black flats. I can't take a chance wearing heels. I surely don't want to tumble down the steps along with her. I feel surprisingly calm as I climb into my car. Destination, Old Town Alexandria, where Annabelle owns a condo. It's about an hour drive from Manassas, where I live. I was so excited when I purchased an end unit townhouse. The only thing that Annabelle said was, "Well, I'd never live here." She then proceeded to trip up the stairs heading to the third floor, spilling an entire glass of Cabernet Franc on the freshly painted white wall. "Thank God it's a foreclosure," she laughed. I should have pushed her down the steps then.

**

My mind wanders back in time as I drive along I-66 East. For our sixteenth birthday, our parents bought us a used, red Dodge Shadow to share. Annabelle whined incessantly if she had to be a passenger, therefore I road shot gun quite a bit.

"What time is drama club over?" She asked. After the Pocahontas fiasco, I had given up on actually being in the play but I helped out behind the scenes.

"Six o'clock. I promised Amanda we'd give her a ride home, too."

"Which one is Amanda?"

"She's the lead in our play."

"Oh, that artsy- fartsy chick. Why do you hang out with such freaks? You know you'd be a little more popular if you dropped all those drama dorks."

"I like my friends because they're not afraid to be themselves. Unlike your fake friends who all look like they've just escaped from a pastel and preppy GAP clothing commercial."

"Because what you wear is much more stylish." She flicked my corduroy jacket. "And you should really wear foundation to cover your mark. You'd be prettier because you'd look more like me."

I stared out the window as hot tears ran down my cheeks. She didn't notice nor did she apologize.

**

As I knock on her door, a pine Christmas wreath dressed in red and gold balls shakes. I feel a pang of guilt when I think about

Annabelle spending the holidays recuperating in a hospital bed. The guilt diminishes as soon as she flings open the door. She's wearing a shiny candy apple red dress, her dark hair is piled high on her head, and pearls hang from her ears and neck.

"Would you like to wear something from my closet?"

"No, thanks." I force a smile. I have to play nice with her until she's standing at the top of the stairwell. At least she's making this easy.

I join her at the bar where she pours each of us a glass of Pinot Noir. "I may as well give you the holiday bag early." She hands me a large silver bag brimming with glittery tissue paper. I gingerly pull out a 2011 calendar with Annabelle's face plastered on the front.

"There are lots of other goodies in there too."

"Thanks." I take a large sip of wine.

"Did I mention that this wine is from Canada? A client brought back a few bottles of this from Niagara on the Lake as a thank you. What a phenomenal gift."

I think it tastes like dirt.

As she rambles on about how fabulous she is, I amuse myself by thinking of other ways to hurt her.

"Would you like another glass of Pinot?"

"No thanks."

"Are you more of a wussy white wine drinker?" She laughs.

I refuse to fight with her. "Are you ready for dinner?"

"Yes, I made a reservation at a new seafood place."

"Fabulous." I smile. She didn't ask about my short story which I hadn't brought in the first place. On the slim chance that she had asked to read it, I would have lied and explained that I left it in the car.

Fortunately, she has to pee before we leave, therefore I have time to snatch one of her stilettos and loosen the heel until it nearly breaks.

My hands shake as I wriggle into my plaid winter pea coat. All I needed was motivation, a little trigger. I stand by the door willing myself to go through with my twisted plan. I won't be content if she twists an ankle, I want broken bones.

"Stop looking so serious. God, you're such an Eeyore. If you were more lighthearted, maybe you'd have a boyfriend." Perhaps she was an effective motivator after all.

I stand off to the side while she locks up. I make sure to follow close behind her and before she takes that first step, I call out her name. "Annabelle."

"What?" She turns and that's when I shove her, a lot harder than I mean to. Her mouth forms a soundless 'O' and her arms actually flail as she falls, just like a cartoon character. When I hear the thud her body makes when she hits the bottom, I scream but it's not soundless. I race down the steps and check her pulse. "Damn it, Annabelle, you won't let me do anything right!"

***

The next few hours come and go in a blur. The police ask a plethora of questions and I do my best to answer but I feel numb. The fact that Annabelle had consumed several glasses of wine and was wearing a defective stiletto adds to the accidental component.

***

I insist on telling Grandpa. This time when I enter his room, he is sitting upright in the recliner and the TV is blaring but he's asleep. "Grandpa, wake up. It's me, Ericka." I shake him gently as if he is a moth with fragile gray wings, lost without light.

"What?" It takes him several moments to recognize me. "Well this is a pleasant surprise." He smiles.

I slide into a chair next to him and grasp his hands. "I have something to tell you."

"Who died now?"

"Annabelle fell down a flight of steps."

"You did it," he says flatly, as if he is a battery with limited juice. He lets go of my hands.

"Grandpa, it was an accident."

"Blood is never an accident or an enemy." He waves his hand as if dismissing me.

"But you said that she was an enemy."

"If I did it's because I'm ninety –seven- years- old, for Christ's sake. I don't know what I'm saying half the time. I was wrong, it's you that's *off.*"

I gasp.

"I won't tell anyone."

"It really was an accident!"

I get up slowly and back out of the living area.

***

And he never did tell. He died at the age of one hundred and was buried with my thirty year old secret, when all along it should have been my secret alone to take to the grave.

What Caught My Senses

Mick slams his fist on Katie's mahogany, Victorian style desk, spilling her cappuccino. "Sugar lips, I have an idea."

"Damn it, Mick. You're lucky this is just a rough draft." She blots the notepaper with tissues.

"If you utilized your computer, like any other sane writer living in the 21st century, then you wouldn't have to worry about soggy paper."

Katie snorts. "No, just a fried keyboard. And I use my computer to blog."

"Regardless, get out your red pen, darling, it's time to brainstorm."

"First, you're going to make me a new cappuccino, please, and thank you."

"I could go for an espresso myself. Be right back."

A few moments later, he returns with their beverages. When he hands Katie hers, she grins. "Juicy, you make the best cappuccinos."

"I know." He sits in the recliner and crosses his legs. When he takes a sip of espresso, he points his pinky in the air.

Katie refrains from calling him 'gay,' because it's a sore spot for him, considering men flirt with him on a weekly basis. In fact, when they met, seventeen years ago, Katie assumed he was gay.

***

"Check out the new guy," Katie's friend Rachel said. They were in the kitchen slicing lemons and Katie nicked her finger with a knife.

"Feck, this lemon juice stings. Yeah, he's cute but he's gay, Rachel. I have keen gay-dar."

"You really think so?"

"Mmm, hmm." She sucked on her finger.

"Eww, Katie, you need a band aid."

"No, I don't. It'll stop bleeding soon."

"But people are going to put those lemons in their iced teas."

"Here you go, darling," the new guy said. He handed Katie a band aid.

"Thanks."

When he was out of earshot, Rachel said, "He's hot."

"He's okay I guess, but did you notice his snaggle tooth? And he has pasty skin, and gangly limbs like a spaghetti noodle. Plus he has a dirty vibe, like he's a skater boy or something. He probably listens to Metallica. And let's not forget, he plays for the other team."

"Geez, Katie. Remind me never to get on your bad side."

She smirked. "Why the new boy isn't on my bad side, silly. He gave me a band aid."

***

Mick watches Katie slurp her cappuccino. He can't believe they've been together since they were sixteen-years-old. At first he thought she was a pretentious princess, which she is, but she's so much more than that. He was immediately attracted to her, even though she was bleeding all over the lemons. Like the other banquet waitresses at the country club, she was wearing a hideous white nursing dress. Katie however, had style. Katie's makeup was perfection, as if she visited a MAC counter at the mall prior. She wasn't skinny by any means, in fact some would describe her as thick, but Mick preferred voluptuous women. And even though their manager frowned upon accessories, Katie rocked pink headbands, dangly earrings, and bangle bracelets.

Mick's goal was to kiss the glittery lip gloss off of her, and eventually, he did.

***

After they finished their beverages, Mick starts his usual pace across the den. "Alright Katie, take notes because I know a way that we can make cash fast." His eyes glaze over like a cashier on National Donut Day, Katie thinks. She scribbles this line on a separate sheet of paper because it might be good enough for a line in her next short story.

"Let me interject. If it includes another round of pet sitting, I'm out. Some of my clothes still smell like cat urine even after I used copious amounts of fabric softener…"

"Shh. Less talking, more listening. We need roughly $2,000 for an editor, correct? What if we offered a writing retreat and charged ten people $200 apiece?"

"But what do we know enough about to teach?" Katie says.

"It doesn't matter. You know how writers are. Most of us are desperate to learn *anything* about writing."

Katie purses her lips. "But we'd have to feed them breakfast, lunch, and dinner. Plus we don't have enough rooms to accommodate ten people."

"That's a good point. I was originally thinking a weekend retreat but we could make it a five day retreat. If we charged $400, we'd only need five writers to attend."

Katie adds this information to her notes. "Five is a much more manageable number. Have you thought of a theme?"

Mick continues to pace across the hard wood floors. 'Writing for Dummies?'"

"No, we attended something similar before, remember? I think it was in Pittsburgh in the late 90's. Plus there's already a book written on that subject." She leans back in her plush desk chair and closes her eyes.

"How about 'How to Write a Novel in Five Days?'" Mick says.

"Just be quiet for a few minutes, Juicy. Let me talk this through. What do we know a lot about? On my blog, I focus on book reviews, writing tips, guest authors, and my weekly post called 'What Caught My Senses.' That's it, Juicy, that's it!" Her eyes grow as wide as plums.

"Care to elaborate?"

"If we offer a five day retreat, we can focus on the importance of sensory detail in regards to writing. Each day we'll feature a sense."

Mick walks behind Katie's desk and kisses her on the forehead. "Sugar lips, you are amazing."

***

Exactly one month later, 'The What Caught My Senses,' retreat begins. Katie and Mick lounge in Adirondack chairs on their front porch, sip fresh lemonade, and wait for their six participants. They decided to invite their friend Rachel as a guest speaker. She was a successful chef, so she'd help with the taste and smell senses. Rachel also offered to pick up and drive the participants to their home, which was fortunate because they lived in the sticks; therefore visitors often got lost and frustrated.

"Here they come." Mick says, as Rachel's Toyota 4-Runner crests the hill.

Katie squeezes his thigh. "Juicy, we've got this."

"I'd prefer if you called me by my given name this week. And don't grab my thighs or buttocks, it's unprofessional."

"That goes the same for you. No boobie fondling."

Mick sighs. "It's a deal."

After Rachel parks her vehicle, the participants climb out.

"Wow, we've got circus animals staying with us this week," Mick says.

Katie giggles. "Let's help them with their luggage."

Mick follows Katie down the steps and walkway.

"Hi, I'm Katie Tumbler, and this is my husband Mick. Please let us help you with your luggage."

After the luggage is delivered to the guest rooms, and the participants use the restroom to wash up, they gather at the dining room table.

"Welcome everyone. Let's start by introducing ourselves. And feel free to eat and drink at your leisure. I hope y'all enjoy barbecue." Katie says, motioning to the elaborate spread. Wow, they really did resemble circus animals, she thinks. "Mick, why don't you start by telling us a little about yourself?"

He puts down the pork slider he was nibbling on. "Sure. As you all know, my name is Mick Tumbler. Three years ago, as part of my thirtieth birthday present to myself, I quit my job as a professor at Webster-Wallace University to write full time. So far I've written five novels, all in the science fiction genre. If any of you brought one of my novels with you, or if you'd like to purchase one or all of my novels, I'd be glad to autograph them for you. Katie?"

"Hello, everyone, I'm Katie Tumbler. Besides a brief stint as a waitress, the only job I've been fortunate enough to have is writing. I write Young Adult novels, in the dystopian genre and short stories. I've written three novels and two short story collections. Like Mick's, all of my novels are for sale, and of course I'll autograph them. Rachel, your turn."

With her pale skin and short, spiked blonde hair, Rachel has always reminded Mick of a cockatoo, and ironically they're often used in circus acts. "Hi, I'm Rachel, the lady who drove all of you here." She smiles. "I'm actually not a writer but the executive chef at The Ivy Stone restaurant. I've known these two successful authors for seventeen years, and I was flattered when they asked if I'd serve as a guest speaker. I mean, who wouldn't want to spend five days in this amazing house? Who would like to go next?"

A young man raises his hand. "Hi, I'm Dave," he says quietly. Dave resembles an elephant with his floppy ears and long nose. "Currently I'm a manager of a coffee house. I'm halfway through my second fantasy novel. That's about it. Oh, and I bet MTV would feature this house on their show *Cribs* because this house is *sick*."

"My name's Pete," the man next to Dave says. "I'm a retired truck driver and I enjoy reading and writing poetry. My favorite poet is Robert Frost." Pete was the spitting image of an old sea lion; plump with thick, white whiskers.

The woman next to Pete resembled the Cowardly Lion from *The Wizard of Oz*. "I'm Victoria and I teach high school journalism. When I'm not teaching or writing poetry, I love to shop, especially for shoes. And I agree with Rachel, your house is breathtaking. I'm really excited to be here."

"I'm Shelby and this is Sheila. In case you can't tell, we're twins." Now that we have identical horses, our circus is complete, Mick thinks. "We're majoring in creative writing at Webster-Wallace University. It's too bad that you don't work there anymore, Mr. Tumbler." Shelby laughs, exposing large, white teeth. Whereas Sheila hides her smile behind her hand.

Katie claps her hands. "I'm so glad that each of you could join us. We're going to have a fabulous five days of fiction writing; now that's alliteration at its finest. While you all eat up, I'll pass out housekeeping tidbits and an outline of events." Katie hands each participant a light green sheet of paper which reads:

Welcome to The Tumbler's First Annual
'What Caught My Senses' Retreat

Bedrooms/Bathrooms

Shelby and Sheila, Victoria and Rachel, Pete and Dave will share rooms. There are extra pillows and blankets in the closets. Each bedroom has an attached bathroom. Each bathroom has a linen closet with towels, wash clothes, and any toiletries that you may need.

Meals

Meals will be served buffet style.
Breakfast: 8-9 am
Lunch: 12-1 pm
Dinner: 6-7 pm

Events

Senses Presentation: 9-12 pm (Monday- Taste, Tuesday- Smell, Wednesday- Touch, Thursday- Sound, Friday- Sight)
Free Write: 1-3 pm

Break: 3-4 pm (Walk the 10 acres, read in the library, relax in the hot tub, nap, etc.)
Free Write: 4-6pm
Critique Session: 7-9pm

"Are there any questions?" Katie says.

"I'm allergic to peanuts and shellfish, and I'd rather not be poisoned while I'm here." Shelby says.

"Rachel, please note Shelby's allergies. Any other questions or comments?" Katie says.

Pete scratches his chin whiskers. "There isn't an event listed for Sunday evening. Are we going to critique each other's work tonight?"

"We thought you would rather settle in tonight, maybe participate in some silent reading or writing," Mick says.

Katie glances at Mick and frowns. "Pete, I think that's a fabulous idea. This evening we'll critique away."

After dinner, Mick cups Katie's elbow and whispers in her ear. "Sugar lips, why'd you shoot me a death look earlier?"

"These people paid a lot of money to be here, and we have to give them what they want, Mick. Your remark sounded like you were brushing Pete off like a fly."

He cracks his knuckles. "I'm already feeling anxious and we haven't gotten through one evening."

"Just relax, let me do all of the talking, I'm good at it." She smiles. "Why don't you whip up some coffees so that we can get started? And then please help Rachel with the clean up."

Katie rejoins the group. "When we critique, please mention the senses utilized in the work. Pete would you like to share your work first?"

He adjusts his glasses and smoothes a piece of notebook paper. "I've written quite a few haikus. This one's one of my favorites:

Around the bend lies
a beautiful lost soul with
tantalizing eyes."

"Excellent. Does anyone have any feedback for Pete?" Katie says.

Victoria tosses her blonde mane behind her back. "I would say the sense of sight as well as touch, because it touches my heart. That one really sings, Pete. If you were a student in my class, I'd give you an A for amazing."

Pete blushes. "Why thank you, Victoria."

"Anyone else?" Katie says. When no one responds, she says, "It flows well, and it utilizes the traditional five syllables, seven syllable, five syllable format, although haikus are often about nature. Overall, good job. Who's next?"

Mick and Rachel bring in a tray of coffees and join the others at the table.

Victoria says, "I also have a haiku to share:

> Children biting the
> tangy flesh of caramel
> covered apple bliss."

"Great imagery, Victoria. In my mind I can clearly see the children, sitting on a bench, swinging their legs, on a pleasant autumn day," Katie says.

"I think it's very sensual." Shelby says, focusing on Mick. "Clearly, the sense of taste is used." She licks her lips.

Katie glances at Mick but he isn't paying attention to Shelby, he's too busy adding sugar to his coffee.

"Thanks everyone," Victoria says.

"Since I have a poem as well, I'll go next," Shelby says. "It's called 'Superficial.' In my original poem, I name dropped but my poetry professor said that was trademark infringement or something, so I made up product names." She rolls her eyes.

"What do you mean by 'name dropping'?" Rachel says.

"I used actual brand names, like Pantene Pro-V Shampoo."

"Yeah, those laws can get sticky, I tend to agree with your professor," Mick says. "Is it by any chance Professor Knight?"

"Yes, that's him. He's like ancient. Anyway, here it goes." She stands up and thrusts out her chest.

> "Low Fat Mayo Shampoo,

for hair so healthy it gleams!
conditions my stringy,
cigarette scented hair and
Lemon Squeezing Hair Color
changes its dishwater hue to
a gorgeous bottle blonde

My lashes look natural, only
richer by adding clumps of
Activated Charcoal Mascara,
because maybe it's natural
or maybe it isn't!

And my skin absolutely glows
with Simply Cocoa Butter
Foundation which evens out
my skin tone and covers zits

Beet Juice Lipstick
is a must for turning
thin, pale lips to a very
natural hooker red

After society has so
conveniently painted my flaws,
I am encouraged to tan with a
fifty-dollar a month package at
Locks Off, Tan On for a
subtle burnt orange hue

Then I head off to the university gym,
for at this point I can't afford
Buns Bunny fitness,
where I struggle to
Keep Calm and Plank On

And do not forget the minor
necessities, lacey push up bras
from Heather's Hush-Hush,

pedi's from Fred's Foot Fetish,
Body Butter Lotion from Mom's Fridge,
and a closet full of Thrift Shop Threads

But I admit, I like looking like a
Shelby doll, after I wake in the
morning with crusty eyes
complete with dark circles,
stubble legs, and chipped nails
I sigh, grab a mascara, and
thank mother nature for makeup!"

When she finishes, she takes a bow, and everyone claps.

"That wasn't facetious at all." Mick grins. "You touched upon a variety of senses: sight, touch, scent, taste, and I would even say sound, considering you used various inflections in your reading. Bravo."

"Makes me glad I'm not a woman," Pete says.

"Amen, brother," Dave says.

"Who hasn't read yet?" Katie says.

Sheila and Dave raise their hands.

"Ladies first," Dave says.

"If its okay, I'd rather not read aloud," Sheila says. She passes out copies of her poem titled "The Exquisite Corpse."

My flamingo pink pants
waltz over to your silhouette
And with groping fingers
you reach towards my chest
yanking the buttons off my
flimsy sweater
Pulling the cigarette out of my mouth,
placing your soft tongue there
You lead me through the hotel door,
and our bodies fall into the
swimming pool with a crash-
like a salacious symphony
composed in ecstasy

"This one caught my sense of touch, that's for sure. The third stanza is my favorite," Rachel says.

Sheila hides most of her face behind her hands.

"And sight and scent is used as well. The opening stanza brings the reader in right away," Victoria says.

"Sheila, were you spying on Raoul and me?" Shelby says.

Sheila's mouth drops open.

"Alright, moving on, Dave, you're up," Katie says.

"I might as well read a poem, too. Actually this is the only poem I brought. It's called 'Rain' and I apologize in advance because it's not very good."

"No one's here to judge you, Dave. We're all here to support you," Katie says.

Dave nods. "Here goes nothing:

'It beats energetically,
it beats softly,
onto the tin can abandoned on the lawn-
full of puddles that children are pouncing in
mud splashing on elated faces

It beats energetically,
it beats softly,
onto the window pane by our bed-
our bodies tangled in sheets,
sweat pouring from elated faces

It beats energetically,
it beats softly,
Beat! Beat! Beat!
Splish! Splish! Splish!'"

"There's beautiful movement in this piece," Sheila says. "My sense of sound was heightened while you were reading that."

Dave blushes. "That means a lot, thank you, Sheila."

"All of your poems are wonderful. You should be very proud of yourselves." Katie says.

Shortly afterwards, everyone heads upstairs. However, one participant, hell bent on destroying Mark Tumbler, while simultaneously writing a horror novel, sneaks downstairs after their roommate is asleep. It's time to heighten everyone's senses, they think.

Before breakfast, Rachel leads everyone onto the back deck, and after they're seated, she says, "As I mentioned yesterday, I'm the executive chef at The Ivy Stone restaurant; therefore the sense of taste is extremely important to me. I thought it would be fun to experiment a bit with this sense. Breakfast will be served immediately after our experiment. I wanted virgin tongues this morning."

"Too late for that," Pete says which causes everyone to laugh.

Without missing a beat, Rachel continues. "We can identify five flavors with our tongue: sweet, sour, salt, bitter, and *Umami, also referred to as savory. There are five numbered small cups in front of you as well as bottled water, because you'll be rinsing in between each flavor. Please take a drink from the first cup and tell me what flavor you identify with."

"Why this one is sweet," Victoria says.

"Correct," Rachel says.

The next two flavors are salty and sour.

"As you can see, the forth solution is a solid, therefore you're going to chew and coat the mouth with this one."

"Bitter, definitely." Shelby scrunches her face.

"Yes, that one is unsweetened baking chocolate. Make sure to rinse your mouth thoroughly. Now take the fifth cup and pour a small amount in the first three cups. Then, take a sip from cup number one. What changes?"

Sheila puckers her lips. "Now it's sickeningly sweet."

At the end of the experiment, Rachel says, "Isn't it interesting how adding small amounts of the Umami increase the salt and sweet sensation but dull the bitter and sour?"

"Thanks, Rachel. That was really interesting. A breakfast buffet is set up in the dining room. Afterwards, Mick and I will teach you how to bring the sense of taste into your writing." Katie glances at the sky. "Looks like a storm is approaching."

Shelby wraps her hands around her throat and starts to wheeze.

"Rachel, were there any nuts in the baking chocolate?" Sheila says.

Rachel shakes her head.

"Well, my sister's having an allergic reaction from *something*. Shelby, is your injector in your purse?" Sheila says.

Shelby nods.

Sheila leaps from the table and runs into the house.

Victoria puts her arm around Shelby. "You're going to be okay, sugar. I know it's hard, but try your best to relax."

"Should we call an ambulance?" Mick paces across the deck.

"I don't know." Katie wrings her hands.

Sheila returns with a tube. She removes the cap, and plunges the needle into Sheila's thigh, where it remains for ten seconds. Then she removes it. "How close is the nearest hospital?"

"About ten miles," Katie says.

"I can drive her. Let me grab my keys," Rachel says. She races to the front door, grabs her keys from the key holder next to the door, and runs back outside.

"Let's go." Sheila attempts to lift her sister but Pete steps in and easily scoops Shelby into his arms.

The entire group heads to Rachel's vehicle.

Pete helps Shelby into the back seat and Sheila squeezes in next to her.

Rachel jumps into the driver's seat. "We'll call you from the hospital once Shelby's settled."

"Remember to call the house phone," Mick says.

Rachel turns the key but nothing happens. "What the hell?"

"Open the hood," Mick says. "I don't know much about cars. Does anyone else?"

Pete shoots him a look. "Let me take a look." Pete fiddles with the engine for less than a minute before he says, "Everything looks fine here."

"Shit," Rachel says. "All the wires have been cut!"

Wires dangle beneath the steering wheel.

"Oh my God," Katie says.

Mick grabs Katie's arm. "Check your car."

"I need my keys." She runs into the house. Less than a minute later, she returns.

"Here's yours." She tosses a set of keys to Mick. Katie's hands shake as she pushes the unlock button and opens the door. When she sees the wires, she screams.

After Mick checks his car he says, "What the f!"

"Call an ambulance for Shelby!" Sheila says.

"I'll call," Rachel says, heading for the house.

"Why don't our freaking cell phones work?" Victoria says.

Dave runs his hands through his brown hair. "Because we're out in the f-ing middle of nowhere. What are we going to do?"

No one responds.

When Rachel returns, she's crying. "The phones are out. I checked both of them."

"Obviously, our first priority is Shelby," Pete says. "Let's bring her into the house."

"Don't touch her! I don't trust you!" Sheila says.

Pete puts his hands in the air. "Calm down, miss."

"Here, let me," Dave says. He picks up Shelby and carries her into the house, with Sheila following closely behind.

"Let's all go back inside. Clearly there's some kind of psycho path out here." Mick says.

"Unless it's one of us," Pete says.

"Pete, that's not funny." Victoria frowns.

"I wasn't joking," Pete says.

"Mick's right. Let's go back inside," Katie says.

They follow her into the living room. Shelby is lying on one end of the oversized couch, wheezing.

"How's she feeling?" Katie says.

Sheila places the back of her hand on Shelby's forehead. "She feels warm and her breathing's off. We need to take her to the hospital."

"What are our options?" Victoria says.

"We'll have to walk to get help. How far are your closest neighbors?" Pete says.

Mick sighs. "Ten miles."

"Ten miles? Why that's going to take a few hours. We better leave now. Who wants to come with me?" Pete says.

"It should only take about an hour if that, we have mountain bikes," Mick says.

"Isn't there a psychopath outside?" Victoria says.

"I tend to agree with Pete. I think it's one of us." Dave says.

"Then how are we supposed to trust Pete? How are we supposed to trust *anyone*?" Victoria says.

Pete throws his hands in the air. "You've got to be kidding me. Well, I'm leaving and either Katie or Mick has to come with me, since I don't know this area."

"My wife isn't going anywhere. I'll go," Mick says.

"Umm, guys, it's pouring outside." Rachel says, staring out the window.

"Then we'll wear raincoats," Mick says. He pulls two raincoats and a back pack from the coat closet. He tosses a few bottles of water and energy bars in the backpack.

"Juicy, please be careful." Katie wraps her arms around Mick.

"We'll be back before you know it." He kisses her on the forehead and then he follows Pete out the door.

"I don't feel well." Victoria is curled on the couch in a fetal position, clutching her stomach.

Katie places a small garbage can in front of the couch and hands Victoria a can of ginger ale. "The soda should settle your stomach."

"Thank you," Victoria says before she vomits in the can.

Sheila is the next to throw up, then Shelby, Rachel, and Dave.

"Oh my God! What is wrong with everyone? It can't be food poisoning, since no one's eaten anything. Is it the flu?" Katie says.

"It must have been the experiment," Dave says. He cradles his head in his hands.

Victoria grimaces. "Rachel, what did we drink this morning?"

"It was just water, sugar, salt, baking cocoa, cream of tartar, and mushroom. I've done that experiment a dozen times and no one has ever gotten sick," Rachel says.

"Katie's fine and she didn't drink anything," Dave says.

Victoria's eyes grow wide. "Have we been poisoned?"

"I bet it was Pete. There's something off about him," Sheila says.

"He's a former truck driver, so of course he'd know which wires to cut in the cars," Dave says.

"Oh my God! I have to find Mick!" Katie puts on her tennis shoes and a rain coat. When she flings open the door, Pete's leaning on Mick and obviously hurt.

"What happened?" Katie says.

Mick helps Pete to the couch. "All of a sudden, Pete felt dizzy. He passed out and on the way down must have twisted his ankle. What the hell is wrong with everyone else?"

"Everyone's sick. We think we've been poisoned," Katie says.

Mick frowns. "You're sick, too?"

"No, I feel fine," Katie says.

"It must have been the experiment," Mick says. "If we're the only ones that aren't sick. I've got to get help." He heads for the door and Katie follows him.

"No, don't leave me here!" Katie says.

"Why?" Mick says.

"Mick," she hisses, "someone here is trying to hurt us. Please don't leave."

Mick sighs. "Okay, I won't leave but what are we going to do?"

"We'll just take care of everyone," Katie says.

But when they return, Shelby and Pete are the only ones in the living room.

"Where's everyone else?" Katie says.

"They have diarrhea now," Pete says.

"How are you feeling? Can I get you anything?" Katie says.

"Water and some pain medicine," he says.

"I'll get it," Mick says.

"Bring water for Shelby, too," Katie says. "How are you feeling, sweetheart?"

"I'm okay," Shelby whispers.

Then they hear a piercing scream and a loud thud.

"What the hell?" Katie leaps from the couch. When she reaches the stairs, she finds Dave lying at the bottom.

"What happened?" Katie says.

"Someone pushed me," he says.

"Mick, help!" Katie says.

Mick jogs down the stairs. Then he helps Dave to a couch. Dave's leg is twisted at an unnatural angle.

Within minutes, Sheila and Victoria return to the living room.

"We all have to stick together," Katie says.

Victoria points at Mick. "It's you. You cut the wires, you poisoned us, and you pushed Pete and Dave!"

"No, I didn't," Mick says.

"Then why were you upstairs?" Victoria says.

Mick dangles a bottle of pain medicine. "I had to grab this from the medicine cabinet."

"Everyone just needs to calm down," Katie says.

"That's easy for you to say. You haven't been poisoned or pushed down a flight of stairs," Victoria says.

"Katie, let's walk for help," Mick says.

"We can't leave everyone in this condition and you're not going alone." Katie puts her hands on her hips.

"Why do I feel like I'm the main character in a horror novel?" Mick paces across the living room.

Victoria gets up from the couch. "I have to use the rest room again," she says.

"Me, too," Sheila says.

Katie nods. "How's everyone doing?"

"I'm still waiting on the pain meds," Pete says.

Katie hands Pete several pills. He pops them in his mouth and swallows.

"Here Dave, you probably need a few, too," Katie offers.

"I'm not taking any pills, I don't trust you," Dave says.

"They're only generic Ibuprofen," Katie says.

"No, thanks." Dave grits his teeth.

"Suit yourself."

"Rachel, how are you?" Katie says.

"I've been better but I'll survive," Rachel says. "I'm worried about Shelby. Are you okay?"

Shelby nods weakly.

And then the lights go out.

"Not only am I in a horror movie, but a predictable one," Mick says.

"We have to make sure Victoria and Sheila are okay. I'll grab flashlights," Katie says.

"Katie, you need to read more Stephen King novels. In a situation like this, separating is the worst thing to do," Mick says.

Victoria returns to the living room and sits in the middle of the couch.

"Where's Sheila?" Shelby asks.

"I'm right here, sis." Sheila walks into the room carrying Mick's hunting rifle in one hand and a duffel bag in the other. "Mick, are you bored? I heard you say something to that effect." She points the gun at him.

Victoria and Rachel start crying and Pete and Dave's mouths drop open.

Katie steps in front of Mick. "Sheila, please put down the gun."

"Sit down, Sugar Lips. You too, Juicy," Sheila says. Mick and Katie share a loveseat.

"Sheila, what's going on? What's that smell?" Shelby's breathing intensifies.

"This isn't your concern, so you can just shut the hell up. And don't worry about the smell," Sheila says. She turns to Mick. "I agree with you, Mick, this horror novel was becoming a bit too predictable. I had hoped that either you or Pete would have stepped into one of the booby traps." She pouts. "Or that a fight would have broken out. Oh well, my game will spice things up."

"W-w-w-why are you d-d-doing this?" Katie says.

"B-b-b-because I can." Sheila laughs, exposing her large teeth. "No, actually I do have a reason but I'm not going to share that right now because that would take away the mystery element, don't you think, Professor Tumbler?"

"Yes, I suppose it would," Mick says.

"Sis, please take a pill," Shelby says.

"I don't need any medicine, Shelby." Sheila tosses her an inhaler. "But please puff away because your wheezing is really freaking annoying."

Shelby takes several shaky breaths from the inhaler.

"Alright, so it's time to play my game. I have to come up with a title for it." She frowns. "Regardless, Katie and Mick, you're the contestants and I of course am the host. I'm going to ask you a series of literary questions. When you answer incorrectly, I desecrate one of your things. When you answer correctly, I don't."

"This is crazy and you're crazy. I'm not playing any of your sick games," Mick says.

"Mick, do what she says," Katie says.

Sheila points the gun at the large screen TV and pulls the trigger. The screen shatters.

"Okay, I'll play," Mick says.

"Victoria, please come here. I need your help," Sheila says.

Victoria gets up from the couch and walks slowly towards Sheila. Mascara streaked tears cover her face. "Please don't hurt me," she says.

Sheila rolls her eyes and hands Victoria a stack of cards. "You're job is to read these questions. Think you can do that?"

Victoria nods.

"Alright, ask Juicy the first question," Sheila says.

"What is the best selling novel of all times?" Victoria says.

Mick cracks his knuckles. *The Bible.*

"Bzzt. That's wrong. The correct answer is *Don Quixote*," Sheila says. She reaches into the duffel bag and pulls out a flash drive and a hammer. "I hope you saved your work elsewhere, Juicy." Sheila pulverizes the flash drive with a hammer.

Mick moans.

"Next question is for Katie. Go ahead, Victoria."

"Who was the first American poet?" Victoria says.

"Oh gosh, I don't read much poetry," Katie says.

"Take an educated guess," Sheila says.

"Umm, Walt Whitman?" Katie says.

"Bzzt. The correct answer is Anne Bradstreet. 'Thou ill-formed offspring of my feeble mind'" (1). Sheila plucks Katie's composition notebook from the duffel bag. "You really need to get on board with technology, Sugar Lips." Sheila strikes a match and lights the book on fire.

Katie starts to cry.

"It's okay, sweetheart." Mick wraps his arms around his wife.

When the book is thoroughly cooked, Sheila drops it on the hardwood floor and stomps out the flames.

"Read, Victoria. Or should I call you Vanna White?" Sheila smirks.

"Which author would take a cold air bath each morning while reading or writing?" Victoria says.

Mick sighs. "Ernest Hemingway."

"Bzzt. Ernest Hemingway did in fact write in the nude but it was Benjamin Franklin who sat in his room each morning naked enjoying the cool air." Sheila pulls a laptop from the bag. She opens it, holds it by the screen, and shakes it. Then she swings it by its cord until it hits the wall and breaks in half.

Mick starts to hyperventilate. Katie gently pushes his head between his legs and coaxes him to take deep, slow breaths.

"How many poems did Emily Dickinson publish during her lifetime?" Victoria says.

"You've got to be kidding me," Katie says. "I don't know, two thousand?"

"Bzzt. Dickinson only published seven poems during her lifetime but she did indeed write nearly two thousand." Sheila pulls a manuscript and a can from the bag. She spreads the pages on the floor and spray paints them black.

Shelby coughs uncontrollably.

"Sheila, please stop. Your sister is really sick. And it smells like there's a gasoline leak," Rachel says.

"Game over. Victoria, I want you to take this duffel bag to the den. Then I want you to light a match. Doesn't matter where you toss it, I poured gasoline on the floor."

"What?" Victoria grimaces.

Sheila points the gun at her forehead.

"Just do what she says," Mick says.

"Be a good girl and listen to Juicy." She hands Victoria a duffel bag and a box of matches.

"I'm really sorry," Victoria says to Mick and Katie before she leaves the living room.

"Would you like to know why I'm doing this?" Sheila says.

"Because you're insane," Dave says.

"I'd be careful with my words, Dumbo," Sheila says. She rests the rifle on her shoulder. "Before you retired, I took a creative writing class with you, Mr. Tumbler. I bet you don't remember me."

Mick shakes his head. "I have a hard time remembering people's names, Shelby."

Sheila grimaces. "My name is Sheila, a-hole."

"I'm sorry," Mick says.

"No, you're not. But it's okay, because neither am I." She sniffs the air. "Victoria, if I don't smell smoke in the next sixty seconds, I'm going to shoot at least one person."

"Look, Sheila, I really am sorry for anything I've done. Please don't take your anger out on these innocent people," Mick says.

The smell of smoke fills the air.

"I've wanted to be a writer since I was five-years-old, Mr. Tumbler. And up until I took your class, my teachers, friends, and family said nothing but positive things. But you..." She clenches her fist. "You called my writing 'mediocre at best,' said my character's problems were 'trivial,' and you compared my writing to a 'flowery, clichéd, Hallmark card.'"

Victoria tip toes into the living room clutching a pair of scissors.

Noticing Victoria, Mick stands up. "But the poem you read last night was anything but flowery. In fact, I thought 'Superficial' was brilliant."

Sheila grits her teeth. "That's my sister's poem."

"How does it feel to be so unmemorable?" Mick says.

"Owwwww!" Sheila moans as Victoria plunges the scissors into her shoulder. Mick wrestles the riffle from her. As Sheila thrashes, Rachel leaps on top of her, pinning her down. Shelby burst into tears.

"Girl fight," Dave says with a fist pump.

"This is the most interesting retreat I've ever been to," Pete says.

"Katie, find something to tie her up with," Rachel says.

Katie runs up the stairs. She comes back with two pairs of handcuffs.

While the women hold Sheila down, Mick places the handcuffs on her ankles and wrists.

"Katie, let's go get some help," Mick says.

"What about the fire?" Katie says.

"I just burned some papers in the trash can," Victoria says.

"Rachel and Victoria, you're in charge. We'll be back with help ASAP," Katie says.

Katie and Mick grab raincoats and bolt out the door. A little over an hour later, they return with several police cars and ambulances. Everyone but Mick and Katie are placed in an ambulance.

"Rachel, do you want us to come to the hospital with you?" Katie says.

Rachel shakes her head. "Rob's meeting me there."

"Okay. I'll call a mechanic concerning our cars. As soon as our phones are fixed that is," Katie says.

While they talk, Mick says goodbye to Shelby, Pete, and Dave. "We'll refund your money, of course," he says. Obviously, he steers clear of Sheila.

After the police officers ask them a plethora of questions, Katie and Mick head inside.

"What an awful day," Katie says.

"It's wine o'clock," Mick says. He pulls half a bottle of white wine from the fridge and pours it into two glasses. They clink their glasses before they gulp the wine.

"Well, I guess we're horror writers now," Katie says.

"That could be the subject of our next retreat." Mick grins.

***

Sheila's lawyer sits in the plastic chair next to her hospital bed. Her wrists are handcuffed to the metal rails and there are two armed police officers standing outside the door.

"You're lucky no one died from that poison," he says.

"It was just eye drops," Sheila says.

"Which is poisonous, especially in large amounts."

On Sunday night, after Sheila poured eye drops in Rachel's experiment, she dumped the rest into the Pinot Grigio in the fridge. She assumed Mick and Katie wouldn't participate in the experiment but wanted them to experience the pleasure of vomiting, at some point. She imagined Katie and Mick drinking the white wine with the tasteless, odorless poison, at that very moment. She hadn't known eye drops could actually kill people. Perhaps Katie and Mick will die! Not such a predictable ending to her horror novel after all, she thinks. She smiles, exposing large white teeth.

\#\#\#

Notes

Bradstreet, Anne. "The Author to Her Book." *The Norton Anthology Literature By Women: The Traditions in English.* Ed. S.M. Gilbert. 2nd ed. New York: W.W. Norton & Co, 1996. 88. Print.

Citriglia, Matthew. Umani-Taste Receptor, Tactile Sensation and Flavor Intensifier. Retrieved from http://www.winegeeks.com/articles/115/umami___taste_receptor _tactile_sensation_and_flavor_intensifier/

"A Fine Winter Day" was published in *The Meadowland Review*, Spring, 2011

"The Collector" was published in *eFiction Magazine*, March, 2012

"Kayanna Pepper" was published in *Backroads Literary Magazine*, Spring 2011

"Motivator" was published in *eFiction Magazine*, September, 2011

About Kristy Feltenberger Gillespie

Kristy Feltenberger Gillespie lives in Warrenton, Virginia with her husband, two cats, and three dachshunds, and they're expecting their first child in July of 2015. Gillespie is a middle school counselor, graduate student at Longwood University, (pursuing a degree in School Library Media) blogger, short story and Young Adult novel writer. When she's not working, she's traveling or dreaming of traveling. She's been on several cross country road trips with her mom. In fact, Hawaii and Alaska are the only states she hasn't been to.

CONNECT WITH KRISTY ONLINE:

Keep Calm and Write On Blog:
http://kristyfgillespie.com

Facebook:
https://www.facebook.com/kristy.feltenbergergillespie

Twitter: @KFGillespie

CHECK OUT KRISTY'S YOUNG ADULT THRILLERS:

Jaded: http://www.amazon.com/dp/B00II0UUSQ

Hunted: http://www.amazon.com/dp/B00UPLMQUG

Blinded: Coming Soon!

www.ingramcontent.com/pod-product-compliance
Lightning Source LLC
Chambersburg PA
CBHW060619130626
46555CB00002B/577